All the Sunshine That Wasn't Grey

RAHUL SHANDILYA

notionpress.com
INDIA • SINGAPORE • MALAYSIA

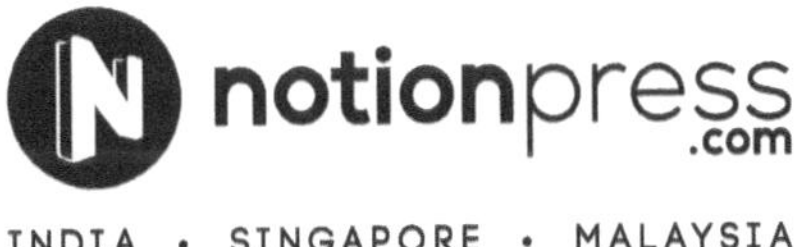

ISBN 979-8-88805-364-5

This book has been published with all efforts taken to make the material error-free after the consent of the author. However, the author and the publisher do not assume and hereby disclaim any liability to any party for any loss, damage, or disruption caused by errors or omissions, whether such errors or omissions result from negligence, accident, or any other cause.

While every effort has been made to avoid any mistake or omission, this publication is being sold on the condition and understanding that neither the author nor the publishers or printers would be liable in any manner to any person by reason of any mistake or omission in this publication or for any action taken or omitted to be taken or advice rendered or accepted on the basis of this work. For any defect in printing or binding the publishers will be liable only to replace the defective copy by another copy of this work then available.

To Mummy, Papa and Chhoti

"One could not count the moons that shimmer on her roofs, or the thousand splendid suns that hide behind her walls."

Khaled Hosseini, A Thousand Splendid Suns

Contents

In the Sky of a Million Stars

1

Like a butterfly, she fluttered in the paddy fields, her arms wide open, her *dupatta* billowing behind her like a cape. As her fingers kissed the dancing, golden, grassy bristles of rice, she scratched her fingertips against her *salwar* to rub off the ticklish imprint. With a *hijab* wrapped around her head, she looked like a sunflower shining in the radiance of a thousand splendid suns. Her hazel eyes squinted into a subjugated wince when she stared at the afternoon sky. *It cleanses the eyes*, she would say. Though seventeen, she had a childlike stammer to her voice, which caused jittery butterflies to bite at the inner walls of my stomach.

Dadi maa had told me her name was Fatima.

November it was. For a lad like me, born and raised in a city, the silence of a village was deafening. I missed the arterial asphalt roads bustling with honking taxis and private cars, flyovers and metros, aesthetic cafés and restaurants which played Bryan Adams and The Beatles on repeat. My days at *Dadi maa's* place were exile.

Ever since I was a toddler, *Dadi maa* had never failed to be the granny from my favourite kid's show—*Baby Looney Tunes.* Be it her dreamy bedtime stories or her delicious, golden brown *gujiyas*, she had so much to fascinate me with. Her messy silver hair would not stop dangling upon her heart-shaped face unless she tied it into a ponytail, which never fell any short of a giant white hamster's tail. Her sunken cheeks made her face bones look bulgy. Her wrinkled, saggy skin and chocolate brown complexion had been the constants throughout. As a kid, whenever papa said she was a young lady once, I would ask him to stop lying.

Papa used to bring her home every winter. She would dare not miss the exotic *Amrapali* mangoes and the *jagrata* season in summers at her village, Kainat. Kainat lay on the outskirts of Ludhiana, Punjab.

We would share my room. I would cuddle inside the blanket, which I wrapped around myself—I hated a plump, running nose. My little face eked out of the blanket as she told me stories. I must have looked cute, for her jagged, misaligned, yellow teeth tore through her lips as she grinned. The child that I was, her smile repelled me as much as her pungent breath.

"Do I look stupid, *dadi?*" I would ask.

"You look like the Caped-Crusader, Abheer," she would say, running her bony fingers through my hair.

"Who?"

She would dive into the story of the Caped-Crusader, a superhero who dressed just like I wrapped myself in the blanket. As legends in her village had it, he lived in the mountains on the outskirts of the country. He could fly, hear what people thought, and beat bad people to a pulp with bare hands. I would tighten the wrap around my face. With a puffed chest, I assumed all the valour of this superhero (because we had this colossal similarity of dressing mannerisms) and went off to sleep.

I talked to her about everything, from a pencil's broken nib to a fellow classmate's funny statement. I could never cross anything she said; my mum could never not exploit that. So it would be *dadi's* job to put me to sleep at nine sharp, *dadi's* job to make me eat mum's much dreaded *tinda sabzi*, *dadi's* job to handle a lousy, cranky Abheer who did not want to wake up for school on most mornings, *dadi's* job again to get my homework done.

Time flows like a river, though, and we drift along. We evolve, or should I say, just grow up? All our relationships must give us that space. They must evolve with us, lest they should break. Sometimes, most of the time, that tension is hurtful. Inevitable, yet hurtful.

When I hit my teens, all my nitty-gritty personal struggles amplified. I was an introvert—the one who always had more to say than he ever would. I was dejected because everyone was not the same as me. They could break promises, say things they did not mean and still have a clear conscience. So I became all the more reclusive, even to *dadi maa*. She kept watching all my transitions with resignation. While I was a variable to time and age, she was a seasoned constant.

One winter, when she came to me, we sat in stark silence amidst the susurrating blower and a tweaking awkwardness in our hearts. Her glimmering eyes roved about my room—it was not the mess it used to be. My *A Song of Ice and Fire* series lay stacked in sequence on the shelf; my *Silvers* racket did not throne on a cluttered pile of course books. My jeans were not crumpled in a heap beneath my bed. My guitar did not have dust lining the tuning pegs.

From my study table, she picked up a metallic, boxy *tabeez* she had tied around my neck at thirteen. "You must never put it off, Abheer. I will take no excuses," she had said. Her gaze would not waver from the *tabeez*, much unlike its pendulating saffron string that hung loose from her palm.

Beside it lay a chestnut brown leather diary, with a quill embossed upon it. She opened the flap to read a note I had addressed to her—to anyone who happened to pick it up. The note read:

This dairy contains my daily schedules and plans, but I may occasionally write confessions I might not like you to read. So in case you have picked it up without asking me, please be good and PUT IT DOWN!

She complied.

If eyes could apologize, mine must have pleaded guilty to her. Although, her propelling ping-pong eyes did not shimmer through her thick, horn-rimmed glasses. Her tender, flaccid lips did not fall at the corners. She did not look away, the way she had when I had thrown my lunchbox out of the classroom window because no one would eat *tinda sabzi* from my tiffin. As if she knew what had come to pass between us. Maybe she did—whenever she asked papa about his clients, the lawsuits he had been dealing in, or simply his day, he always said it was all fine.

I had to go to Mumbai for my undergraduate studies and I could not have the surety of seeing her when I returned. Courtesy: her old age. So I had decided to live with her at Kainat, her village, where she was happy to be in her last days. *Amidst my own people, where the air reeks of the soil I am made of,* she said.

My last visit was not as I had thought it would be. As she could only hear loud sounds, I had to raise my voice to talk to her—not the least bit to my liking. She did not remember anyone, me included, who came to see her, except for select few villagers. For the most part of the day, she would be asleep. I had forbidden her maids from giving her leg massages; she loved how some anonymous helper cracked her toes. I had to stress on her memory so she would let me massage her legs with her all-purpose *Rhuma* oil. My *Dadi maa* not recognizing me! It was not…nice.

A moment of solace was watching Fatima every morning from my bedside window. In the fields, she sprang from the earth like a sparrow. I would often sync her leaps with cooing morning cuckoos. For every beat she missed, I bit my lip or clenched my teeth. Her aura was a beautiful mystery, and my heart ached at what *Dadi Maa* had told me about her. Her facing anything because of some silly belief of this place was blasphemous to the things she made me feel. She deserved…to be loved.

She had come to see *Dadi maa* with her mother—the beauty of villages. She stood at the threshold, pressing against the withered, prickly wooden frame; her mother sat beside *Dadi maa* inside. An orange *hijab* with polka dots all over wound around her head so tight that her cheeks, white like milk, slacked out. Her eyes shamelessly followed the flying fringes as she blew at her hair that had escaped the *hijab*. She was lost in her own world, in a self-declared contest, finicky that those flying strands of hair must never land on her glossy, oval face.

As soon as they left, I rushed to *Dadi maa*'s bedside.

"Fatima is her name," she said, smiling, as if she had sensed my feelings for her. *Dadi maa*!

Through her window, the girl, Fatima, walked away—no popping or staggered movements but mincing footsteps that would not cover more than a quarter of a foot. At an arm's length from her mother, as if an outcast.

"Poor girl is cursed," *Dadi maa* said.

Her eyelids grew heavier and heavier; she dozed off. I sat beside her, in a whirlpool of anxiety, questions, and haunting imaginations.

2

Breaking dawn. A sleepless night. Wandering lonely in the paddy fields.

The sky had hatched; the captive sun was breaking through. Along the fracture, it was red. Beneath it, grey. Golden fused into amber, amber into yellow—the night had reached its climax. Huts with thatched roofs, *dadi's* pukka house with two storeys, trees of coconut, banyan, scarlet and orange Gulmohar with feathery pinnate leaves, all lay in a row like in the miniature toy train cities. The village was waking from its silhouette. As I yawned, my watery eyes disbanded the sunshine into colours of the rainbow.

A few yards away, a girl in avocado-green *kurti* slogged in the fields, her gaze at the ground, hands stretched out like the wings of a jet plane to find balance. I squinted; it was Fatima. No *hijab*; her sea-green *dupatta* sailed behind her like a cape in the morning breeze. But for the paddy, she must have run—she chased something. I trotted towards her, my legs jaded from a sleepless night.

She halted at the field partition. A few steps away, a rabbit with white fur and a black patch slashed across its face nibbled at a wild yellow flower. As her hands advanced towards the rabbit, her shadow must have nudged it. It jumped a step; she froze. It started biting at some weed again.

Fatima had stooped only halfway when the rabbit sprang again. It hopped into the paddy this time. As she sprinted after it, her ankle twisted—she fell. She let out not so muffled groans.

When I offered her my hand, she rejected it with a side-glance—a look of both intimidation and incongruity. In a panic, she flicked at her *dupatta* hanging behind her shoulder. She tied it around her head with fidgety, rushing hands as if I must not see her bouffant brown hair, coiffed with hair clips, falling behind her like a waterfall.

Her toe was bleeding, but she would not take my handkerchief. She would not look up even. She tore a piece from the loose end of her *kurti*, tied it round her toe, and fisted against the ground to push herself up. As she hobbled ahead, she must have bitten her lip—she was caging her groans, perfecting her gait, throwing a gesture in the air that her leg was fine.

Why was I not feeling offended? I must talk to her, but my plight—I had always floundered at initiating conversations and making friends. My words would fizzle when she stared. Fingers crossed!

"Hey! I love rabbits too. Can you find me a similar one as yours?"

Argh! The worst pick up line ever! Her hobbling transitioned into long, fastened strides. It must be hurting…I was hurting her.

"Hey, is your leg fine?"

She shook her head. *Phew!* I yielded to her.

"Please wait," I said, my eyes squeezed. I knew something planned always failed when it came to matters of heart.

"I want to say something to you."

She froze again. Her *kurti* fluttered with the zephyr, but her head would not budge. Her hands, legs, shoulders, fingers, everything frigid, as if she were a scarecrow and not the girl I loved. She would not even turn; she did not want to look at me. Cold sweat dripped from my forehead like water from glassy icicles; the silence was piercing.

"It's not all the time that I bump into someone merely the sight of whom makes me…*umm*…happy. It's not all the time that someone avoids me and I just can't feel offended. It isn't all the time that I feel an urge to befriend someone from within, so strong that an introvert like me doesn't even fumble once while speaking his heart out to you. I don't have many people in this village, or for that matter in my life, who I can talk to. Still fewer when it comes to people I *like* talking to. But you—" I choked to swallow, "—Will you be my friend?" I asked, my eyes squeezed shut, my fingers stiff, my stomach churning.

Awkward silence! She did not turn. The entire candy floss of modesty standards started making sense to me.

It isn't modest of a woman to befriend a man in this way in a village like this. People already have wrong beliefs about her. I should not push things further.

There was a split in my head. I feared I could add to her miseries, but how could I not make friends with her?

Wait, haven't I followed her through a stretch of ten yards? How many people must have watched us? Will they not cook stories about her now? Argh!

She had turned.

"We have met before. Day before yesterday you came to our place to see *Dadi maa.* So we aren't complete strangers." I rushed to fill in words, lest her silence, her misaligned extra canines breaking through her half smile, her gaping hazel eyes should crush me. "I promise you'll not have to bear with me for long. I'll be gone in two months."

Her smile vanished. *God! Choke me dead with her dupatta, please!*

"Why should I make friends with someone I know will not be with me forever," she asked. Her voice had gravity. Glimpses of tormenting loneliness flashed in her eyes, or maybe I was overthinking.

"Because you'll then have a letter to await every month, a letter that will tell you that you have a friend in some far off place who misses you, remembers you, and values you. And I promise one such letter will tell you that your friend is coming back for you. I promise you'll always cherish the letters you await. You'll always have me with you in those letters, if not by your side."

She smiled. Oh god! It was happening. I was breathing better now.

"Fair deal?" I asked.

"*InshAllah!*"

"But I don't know your name."

"*Kulakshani.*" Bad luck, she said.

I swallowed a lump. Perhaps she wanted to give me a reality check. Perhaps she believed it to be her reality. Perhaps, she wanted me to know how being friends with her could impact my social standing. If only I could tell her, without choking, how it did not matter.

She smiled at me again as if she knew it would work.

"Fatima is not that bad for a name." I smiled back. Her lips did not waver, nor did her glance. *Wait! Does she know I was pretending? Telepathy? Huh! I just suck at charades.*

I put forward my hand, but she would not shake it.

"*Ya Allah!* Don't you know, Muslim women do not shake hands with men? Allah forbids physical contact with men other than the woman's *Shauhar,* dumbo," she said, covering her laugh with her calloused fingers. The scratch marks on her hand continued beneath her sleeve like rivulets.

We were talking now.

I did not know when we reached the end of the village. I was lost in Fatima's blabber and her homemade scent of rose and lavender. She had made it all by herself; she even told me the recipe. The sun was up now. There were people on the streets, but she did not seem to care much.

In her own train of thoughts, she went on telling me gossip about the village, limping all the while. I now knew that the *Sarpanch's* son wore track pants that could slip down anytime. The village *Mukhiya* farted in public all the time, and always passed the blame onto his *munim.* She told me so many things but nothing about herself.

Engrossed in the conversation, she did not realize she had reached her home. Fatima lived outside Kainat, with all the other outcasts. Her house, or a shack to say, was the third out of the only four in the line. They must be walking nothing less than a kilometre to buy as much as a toothpaste even.

Her mother must have been a beautiful woman when she was happy. Her slim, hourglass-like body, draped in a grimy, orange *kurti,* jutted from the wooden frame of her door. Her bony fingers covered her V-shaped, oily face below the nose. She was not wearing a *hijab*; she would also rush to find hers if she caught me looking at her hair, the traces of white near her ears. Her eyes, hazel like her daughter's, perhaps vindictive, were not scrutinizing Fatima's new friend from head to toe. They were waiting, rather, to meet *her* eyes.

When they did, she gave her a bitter look. Fatima's lips uncurved. Her gaze would not lift from her dilapidated, leather sandals. A flaccid look conquered her face as if our conversation had been a dream. She did not even say goodbye but galloped with her twisted ankle and entered her house.

Her creaky door slammed behind her. I stood there, watching.

3

I have been lonely. I know how to savour it.

My only friend circle was my best friend at school. Every recess, I played hand-cricket with the very backbencher boys who scribbled on my shirt in class, just so I could be with him. We raced in copying notes from the smart-class screen in every geography class. Of course, he won, every time.

We could only do our vacation projects together if the sessions happened at his place. So I had to walk three kilometres in the afternoons every summer break. I would draw his complicated biology diagrams; he did not ask me to. Why? I wanted him to have reasons to stick with me, maybe. Maybe I feared he would find someone funnier, someone who would bunk classes with him or scribble crisscross games on the desks. He could find a better company, but I would not find another him. I would always make sacrifices. I would not tell him I liked something if he did not. I would always say sorry. I had thought it was friendship.

That summer, when the school resumed, though, the myth broke. When I returned to class after recess, my project file lay on my desk, a *Beyblade* name-sticker layered over the one that bore my name. The nameplate was his; the file had been checked.

As my palm went red with the teacher's agonizing stick, he watched. His *chapri* backbencher friends laughed, but he did not retaliate on my behalf. He watched.

"I had forgotten my file at home," he said after dismissal. That was not an apology, no?

A day passed. He did not come to talk to me.

Another day passed, and another. Waiting was excruciating; the shards of a realization started creeping beneath my skin. Did it even matter to him? For once, will he come for me?

He did not.

If I confronted him, I would swallow my words and hate myself later. So I wrote on a piece of paper and dropped it at his desk before the morning assembly.

If you don't realize what you have done, we cannot be friends.

Later that day, a paper ball popped at my back. FINE, he had written in bold below my one liner.

My luck with friends was not much different in high school either. When I was fifteen, I fell in love. She was beautiful. The world seemed a beautiful place now.

I had started listening to *One Direction*. I could sing the highest notes of *What Makes You Beautiful*, I could do it with a guitar. I had also written my first poem for her, and mind you, it was a fine Shakespearean sonnet.

However, I did not know how to seat her beside me and sing to her while her eyes explored mine. Her smile would shake my voice. How would I hit that high note then? How should I slip that poem into her notebook? Would she understand it? How would I stand her stare if she did?

Although, I had friends for that. Or maybe not. I did not know. They said they were. All I know is that my love was a joke to them. The only person noticing and feeling bad for me was her. She respected me, though she could never reciprocate my feelings. She taught me it was not her fault if she could not feel the same for me.

That was my last shot at friendship. I have always associated love more with longing for people. I start to fuss when they are around. I have been lonely, and I know how to savour it.

One day, though, I asked Fatima about loneliness, and she said, "one morning, when I was twelve, I woke up to blood between my legs and thought I was going to die. I didn't have my *Ammi* to take me in her arms and tell me it wasn't the end of the world."

Her words blew a raspberry at the castle of loneliness I had erected with trump cards.

"I was shivering," she said, "fearing the unknown. I could drench the bedsheet red—I wouldn't stop being a menace to my mother, even in death. Was I to remain awake to every drop of blood leaving my body? Or would death be merciful? Would it let me sleep while it happened? I wanted to weep, but maybe I was dehydrated. I don't know. Pangs of anxiety and incoherent thoughts were tearing through me. I wanted to talk to my mother, but all that would follow was an awkward silence. All I had ever made her feel was wretched, and I didn't want to do it at that moment. It felt cold, as if I were yelling to be saved, but the demonic silence swallowed my screams. And then..." she trailed off.

A heavy breath!

"...my frazzled mind gave way. My mother, my small hut, with beige, earthen floors and thatched roof, its front door that creaked twice in a full arc's swing, the paddy fields, my rabbits, Mullah Fatiullah Sahab who lived two houses away, the *Taiji* from next door who brought me *Pohas*, your *Dadi maa*...everything, seemed to be slipping away. I lay there, too weak to lift a finger or shake a leg. My eyelids were growing heavier each second. The world was closing in on me, and it was getting peaceful—maybe I had yielded to it. As they say, it's only fear that brings with it thunderstorms. Death has always had a tranquil embrace. And then..."

"But...but...but..."

Her finger bridged my half-open lips—a touch as frail as a hummingbird's feather brushing at my lips, coarse as if blades of grass. Her other hand covered a hearty laugh at my silliness.

"When I woke up, I was lying in *Taiji's* lap. She caressed my cheeks, and told me I was a woman now, and I would bleed every month. And that I was special, because I bled to sustain life," she said.

I sighed. Fatima laughed again, except that it was short-lived this time.

She had touched my lips; Allah must be angry. That flaccid look on her face returned. She shifted away from me on the bench, her hands tucked between her thighs. Her eyes stole from me as if I must pretend with her that she had not broken the rule. But she had, and for me. How could I not feel special?

Gosh! How cute she was!

"*Astaghfirullah…*" she said, almost in a whisper.

"What's that?"

"An apology to Allah for my sin."

It was my turn to laugh.

4

"*Beta ji, dheere dheere se malish kariye!*" *Dadi maa* said. I eased my grip, lest her weak legs—a thin sheet of brown, wrinkled skin sticking to the bones at the shin, saggy at the calves—should break like chalk in my hands. At eighty, the muscles in her legs were a petty excuse. She could not walk without her polished, chestnut brown walking staff. The staff also served as atonement for her maids and me—anyone who confronted her for spitting beside her bed, or not calling someone when she wanted to pee, or simply placing her food plate at more than an arm's length from her. It must always lay tucked between the bed and the corner of the room, within her left arm's reach.

Laced in her almighty *Rhuma* oil, my palms wrapped around her frail, bony legs. I started from her knees, descending through her shin, calves, to her favourite part, the feet. Time to ask her!

"*Dadi maa?*" I said as I wrapped my arms around her feet, giving her a long, gliding stroke up the leg.

"*Haan* Abheer?" She said, her voice quivering from the pleasure of my thumbs pressing at her heels, the ball of her foot, her toes.

"What is that curse you talked about the other day? You had said Fatima was cursed."

"*Beta ji*, it's a vicious ritual—the birth curse. *Bhali bachhi hai* Fatima, but the curse is there."

"What is this curse, *dadi*?"

"Once upon a time, Abheer," she said as I cracked her hammertoes. "Kainat had an emperor, Kashthala. He waged war against the four demon brothers—Shaivashya, Bipallatra, Shurprigha and Thrismatra, who had taken a liking to ravaging the empire.

Luckily enough, if you'd call that, Shaivashya fell for Sanghamitra, Kashthala's daughter. None of his brothers liked it, but love is love. When Kashthala learnt about it, the master plotter made his daughter the centre of his plan. Sanghamitra lured Shaivashya into her father's trap; Kashthala took Shaivashya down.

A wave of mistrust hit the three remaining brothers. Each of them started plotting individually, just as Kashthala had anticipated. One by one, he killed each of them, but…"

"…but…" I said, lacing her left foot with oil.

"…but the village believes the evil was far from over. Their demonic spirits are angry, and they return. *Vaishakh mein, har saal.* Each on the same day as they died.

People born in those nights are said to bear 'the birth curse.' They are cursed to bring harm to their families."

"How is it even fair, *dadi*? They have done nothing to deserve this!"

"Very unfair, *par log mante hain. Kya karein?*"

"Do you believe in this?"

"I don't know, but Fatima doesn't deserve what she gets."

"Yes! She doesn't deserve it. She's such a nice girl," I almost screamed. At that, *Dadi maa* smiled.

"*Dadi maa!*"

"*Beta ji!*"

"Nothing! I am done with the massage."

"*Achha theek hai!*" She said, and turned to sleep.

Why is it okay for history and beliefs to destroy lives?

5

"So you tell me that a seventy-year-old man, with a silver beard that hangs down to his chest, is not your Quran teacher but a friend? As in, friend *wala* friend?" I asked as she swept beneath her rump to clear her seat of pebbles.

"Sixty-nine years and five months," Fatima said, spitting each word out as she swirled her eyes around my incredulity. "And Mullah Fatiullah Sahab does not teach me the Quran, mind you. *Ammi* does. He just tells me stories, helps me remember all the teachings through that. And it works like magic for me."

It was half-past midnight in the paddy fields, a chilly, starry one. We sat at the cross of the field partitions, on a patch of wet grass so the frigid earth did not freeze our bases. The air reeked of freshly falling dew, our skin moist from it. Fatima was through with her gossip, blabber and rants.

"So you remember verses from the Quran?" I asked.

"Not everything, Abheer, but yes, a lot of them. I do," she said.

"You remember *a lot of* verses from the Quran?"

"What do you mean? You don't remember things from the Bhagwad Geeta?"

"I haven't read it."

"*Haww*! Abheer! How do you know then what god has to tell you?"

"I mean…*umm*…I attend *pujas* and rituals. I know a fair amount of things from them."

"You know nothing Abheer, *I attend pujas and rituals*," she mewled, mimicking me, cracking into laughter.

Talking to Fatima was like sitting by a lakeside in a moonlit night, just like that one. Fatima was the lake. The trembling, shining water—the chirpy, talkative, happy persona she created around herself—formed a mirror. When I looked into it, I saw my own reflection, as deep within it as I stood away—I was her friend now, just like Mullah Fatiullah, *Taiji*, or my *dadi maa*. The moon—her eyes that gave me death glares if I interrupted her—disintegrated into white, horizontal pastel strokes, forming an oval on the water. The stars, the cityscape, silhouettes of sprawling trees, vigil houses with yellow, sometimes white lights—the beautiful things she made me feel.

Oh, how well the water masked her loneliness—the muddy, sinking terrain of the lakebed that would swallow your feet if you walked into it. The further you went, the deeper you drowned. The water took its shape, filled it to the greatest depths, and created a flat, feeble surface, off which reflected the stars, the moon, the night—a homey facade.

Unless, of course, you threw a stone at it and distorted its stillness.

"What's the point of remembering, if you don't follow it, *eh*?"

"What do you mean, *haan*? I follow everything Allah says," Fatima said.

"*Achha? Toh* Allah allows making friends with a man? And sneaking out every night to sit by his side?" I chuckled, only to realize it was not funny.

Her face wilted like a flower that should not be touched. "You know nothing, *dumbo!* In all my *namaz*, I...I...I plead Allah for forgiveness. He will forgive me..."

You do all this, for me? I ate these words.

"...and what is this *sit by his side*," she mewled again, "I never touch you. See, there is this much distance," she said, oscillating her palm between her waist and mine—a three-fourth of an arm's length.

"But why at night only?" I asked. At that, she gave me a glance, one good stare. I felt stupid.

Fatima plunged into another story, which involved the obnoxious shopkeeper of the nearest grocery store and Tahira, *Taiji's* daughter. Tahira shared her curse, or a milder version of it, maybe. Fatima's list of friends did not include her, so chuck it. Come back to the lake.

When the stone hit the water, it gurgled and sank. The water rippled; the lake became a playground for unnerving, flurrying wavelets—Fatima's awkward glances, daunting silences. The mirror vanished, my reflection with it—her miseries and I existed in parallel dimensions, in separate worlds that she would not let intersect. Every inch of the water shook, but it would not reveal the swamps. I could not perceive the lakebed until I walked into it. And the deeper I went, the harder the water pushed me out with its buoyancy.

"…And Mr. Over-smart didn't say a word after that. Tahira gave a perfect reply to him. I wonder why such people never…"

"Fatima…"

She broke off, giving me her usual death glare. "I want to know who you are," I said, staring into her eyes.

"I'm Fatima Hassan, you *dumbo*," she said, stealing her gaze from me, trying her best to laugh.

"*Ha ha!* So not funny. I am serious, Fatima."

"*Ohho!* Abheer gets serious also. Nice, nice!" Fatima picked a tuft of dry grass from beneath her knee, and started untangling it.

Fatima did not know that *Dadi maa* had dropped me in the middle of that lake. Fatima was born in the night of Shaivashya—the fiercest of all nights. The demon sought direct revenge. People born that night bore the deadliest curse—to kill a person they loved.

But I wanted to hear her story from *her*. For once, I wanted the lake to invite me in.

"I want to know you, Fatima. Ever since I came here, I've heard things about you and all those things torment me. They say you're cursed, but you're the most beautiful…

…I want to know what lies within you. I want to know what your life has been like till now. I want to know you."

Her eyes wetted; the thick sheath of ice had started melting.

"I'm my mother's cursed child, Abheer," she said, "the daughter who killed her father. The night I was born, my father couldn't arrange for midwives. The evil hour! *Taiji* had to handle the delivery. *Ammi* had to endure thrice the usual pain…" She broke off.

"…My father refused to abandon me. The villagers all turned against him, and he fought like a hero.

Ammi says *Abbu* was an honourable man. A man of high morals and rigorously scientific outlook, he was the only *Vaidya* who could treat a heart attack case in the village. The villagers had always respected him. They never really meant to kill him, but…" she sighed.

"…But he dared to question faith," I completed for her. Her vacant stare had fixated on her thumb.

"Voices were raised. *Lathis* were swung. Arguments got heated to the extremity of riot. *Abbu* fought like a hero, but he had to yield to the majesty of faith…

…And then, faith didn't fail them. The curse fell upon *Abbu*," she said.

"But…but…but…it wasn't…"

"My mother believes so."

"This is stupid," I sniffed. It exasperated me to the extent that her death glare fell flat.

"My *Abbu* was the *noor* of *Ammi's* eyes," she continued, "And to *Abbu, Ammi* meant the world. *Abbu* said I would be the emblem of their love."

"But Fatima, it wasn't you," I said.

She looked at me, and her lips curved. "I know," she said. I felt stupid again.

"Someone you love leaving you is sad, Abheer. It hurts. But you know what's worse? It's when you want to isolate yourself, feel deserted and lonely. It is when you want to collect the anger, the broken pieces, and forge your walls with it, but there are people who love you still. Their love does not soothe you, does not heal you, when it should. You push them away, only to feel more wretched, caught up in an ugly middle position. You're crying for love, and pushing it away…"

"…Feelings are bizarre," I managed to speak.

"For *Ammi*, it was my love. I have always made her plight more wretched. I've always broken her…"

Her eyes shot up at the sky above, embellished with stars. For long, she did not notice that I had been looking at her. She was a warrior.

And slowly, the ruffling ripples reached the lakeside, crashed, and died. The water stopped shaking; the fragile mirror returned. The sinusoidal reflection of the moon faded into horizontal, and the stars hovered in the water again. The lake was calm, beautiful and homey, just how it wanted to be.

And when I looked into that mirror again, I saw my own reflection, as deep within it as I stood away.

"You're beautiful," I said.

It stirred her; she turned her head away. However, she failed to hide that faint smile. And the blush maybe, but I could be wrong.

"Mullah Fatiullah has promised me four stories tomorrow," her funky self took over. "He dare not stop after the third or else…"

"*Astaghfirullah*," I interrupted.

"For what?"

"For trying to flirt with you," I smirked.

"No. That was…that was nice. Thank you." She avoided eye contact and barely smiled. As she adjusted her *hijab* with nervous hands, a fringe of her hair fell upon her face.

"So you liked it, *hmm*?"

You could not pull that off on Fatima more than once.

"No, you're stating plain facts." She rolled her eyes at me, and then we both burst into laughter.

"*Huh!* Self-obsessed!"

"Listen, I hate old-school dialogues, but I am my personal favourite," she sniffed.

"*Argh!* I have only ten days of stay left in this village. I've already started missing you." At that, she swallowed a lump, but she did not let the look on her face change.

"We are all to this world like the stars to the sky," she said.

"Are you sure there's no way to talk to you? Like *talk-talk*, not *letter-talk*. No phones in the village? Nothing?"

"You can only write to me."

"*Hmm*. Okay, but please spare some time from your busy schedule and try to reply to my letters. I'll be longing for your replies. Will you, Miss Hassan?" I tried a puppy face.

"I can't promise that, you know. I am a busy woman," she said, breaking into a chuckle.

"And will you please oblige me with another piece of information?"

"*Umm*, depends on what you ask."

"When I come back after years, in my sixties, in my Mercedes, where shall I find you?"

"I'll be alive somewhere. Won't be hard to find, if you give a hearty try, you know?"

"Please oblige me Miss Hassan. Please."

"Find me there," she said, pointing at the sky. "In the sky of a million stars."

With that she giggled. I smiled. We laughed.

6

Fatima pulled the barrel, but the gun did not clink while loading. It was a warm afternoon. Walking by my side, she held the gun at my head. Almost point-blank, but the muzzle could not touch even my hair. With side glances, I could see her caper-smitten eyes half-closed in focus. Her eyelids did not waver as her finger brushed the trigger. Or when she pulled it.

Dhishkiyaoon!

"For Allah's sake, Abheer, can you ever just play along," snapped Fatima, for her imaginary bullet and finger shotgun had failed to budge me.

"Sure," I laughed, "if you make it…*umm*…a little bit realistic?"

"Shut up!" Fatima rolled her naked eyes, the rest of her face draped with an unusually long, scratchy sheet of cloth, which also covered her hair and hung all the way down to her calves.

"I mean, look at those frail, tiny fingers. At max, they can make that *Holi wala* water gun," I crackled again. At that, she stopped walking. I turned, only to see her holding her shotgun close to her right eye, aiming between my legs.

Phissssssssssss!

"What?" I asked.

"Now everyone's gonna think you peed in your pants."

"*Chhee!* Fatima!"

"There we go! Now you're playing along," she burst into laughter.

We must have reached Assi Khurd, a village she wanted to show me, for Fatima removed her veil. The cloth now hung from her head like a shirt from a wall hook.

"Why this village, Fatima?"

"You only crib about the night and the cold. So here, I meet you in broad daylight," she said as she stooped down to pick an arm-long bamboo stick lying at the side of the rugged, probably unadopted road that led into the village.

"So there is nothing special about this village?" I rolled my eyes. "You made me walk twelve kilometres just so you could meet me in the afternoon?"

"Who said there's nothing special?"

"What is special then, tell me?"

"This village lets me feel normal," she said, nonchalantly. Did she even know her mouth was acing at what she so wanted her fingers to be?

As we trod down the road lined with *Rabi* fields on both sides, a marketplace appeared. People appeared. Although, unlike in Kainat, Fatima did not cover her face with jittery, shaky hands. She did not distance her walk from mine or stop talking in the middle of a sentence to pretend she did not know me. Instead, she swivelled to look at me, her eyes prodding that I held the loose end of her stick.

"Is this your version of holding my hand?" I chuckled.

"Do you want me to show you or not?"

"Yes, yes!"

I trailed after her as she jostled her way through a messy throng of people, taking good care not to touch any men, but letting her arms brush, sometimes even nudge the arms of girls and women. Those villagers did not budge at the sight of Fatima. No piercing, frantic, malicious gazes. Buying rations, bargaining with the fish vendor, extracting free *dhaniya* from the greengrocer, and authenticating the spare parts used in their radio, were all more important to them than fussing about Fatima's frugal walk past them. Fatima was not a *Kulakshani* here.

Past the marketplace, we ambled down a bumpy earthen street, lined with single-storey pukka houses on both sides. Their walls were painted with limestone, with algae all over. These houses strictly had a small garden, with jasmine, tomatoes, brinjal etc. And one big tree, mainly mango, whose branches sprang out of the boundaries and shaded the street in patches. Fatima took a turn into the interstitial space between two such houses, so narrow that I had to walk behind her. As I hobbled after her through that space, blades of grass pricked at my feet. I clutched the stick harder.

On the other side, the grass grew in length to knee-size. An abandoned pond, green with algae, lay before us. I staggered after Fatima till we reached the clearing around it. As we neared the pond, she dropped the stick in her hand and advanced towards an old banyan tree just a few feet away from the water. There lay a heap of dry grass in its shade, upon which she clawed until she found what she was looking for—a stack of waste cartons taped together.

It was only when she opened it that I realized—it was taped in a manner to form an igloo, or a kennel, whatever. Fatima swept the ground with her feet, took off her *hijab*, and laid it down to make the floor. Over it, she constructed her cardboard home. When it was ready, she held my hand (as if Allah was not watching) and walked me in.

Inside it, we sat doubled up, our chins digging at our knees. She would not say a thing. For good five minutes, the silence continued before she broke from her posture and hugged me from the side.

"What about…Allah?" I blurted.

"I haven't invited him in," she said, her face as straight as ever. "Nobody is invited here. This is my home, just mine."

"Fatima, what has happened?" I said, in a melted tone.

"Has your mother ever slapped you, Abheer? Has she ever broken a broomstick, actually one and a half, on your body? Has she ever told you she would be much better off if you died, and you couldn't convince yourself she didn't mean it? Has she ever asked you to die, and called you selfish because you're afraid to?"

"*Umm…I…ah…*"

"Then you won't understand."

"Fatima?"

"I love her, Abheer, I love her. I don't know. To her, I've always been her husband's killer. She just…can't love me back. And it's not OK. I don't know. I understand her reasons, none so well as I do. But…it hurts.

I love her, and she loves me too. But she doesn't run her fingers through my hair, doesn't caress my cheek, doesn't listen to my stories, doesn't tell me her own, doesn't teach me how to cook *dal bhati,* doesn't do my ponytail, doesn't teach me how to knit, doesn't celebrate Eid with me…like all mothers do. Don't I deserve that?

She doesn't talk to me unless she's got some work. Even then, she wouldn't *ever* look at me. She doesn't want me to see it. Perhaps she feels I don't deserve it—her love.

She doesn't like my talking to anyone…"

"And last night, she beat you up because you talk to me?"

Fatima nodded.

"I have never seen her happy, Abheer. Sometimes I feel like running away, but she has no one in the world in the name of family, no one but me."

"Fatima…I…" I tightened my arm around her.

"Abheer…*argh*…" she groaned.

"What happened?"

"My back…it's…bruised."

Through the door (if that is what you would call it), the sky had transitioned from blue to orange. We sat beside each other, basking in the silence that had fallen upon us like the dusk outside. Crickets whistled, and mosquitoes hummed. We rubbed off the tiny insects crawling at our feet against the grass. It was getting cold.

"You know Abheer, I sleep with *Ammi* every night. We have only one cot. Every night I feel her, touch her. Every night I'm convinced she's there. You know, when she snores, it puffs in my ear. And you know she has a burn mark just below her right eye. When she was little, she had once tried to burn a polythene bag, and its burning drops had fallen on her face."

"She told you that?" I asked.

"Yes, Abheer. Yes, she told me. Very rare, but sometimes she's not angry with me. You know she had almost lost her eye and gotten good thrashing from *Nani maa*. My *Ammi*! I can stare at her for hours without blinking. My *Ammi* is beautiful, Abheer.

And then she wakes up. Morning happens, and everything becomes a dream," she broke off.

"Fatima, we all have someone we love so much that we want to solve everything for them. But can we? All we can do is love them in our own way. And hope. Hope that they'll find their missing pieces and complete themselves," I said, but she was not listening. She was staring at her thumb again, vacantly.

"I like talking to you," she said, "I spend the rest of my day thinking about our conversations, longing for night to fall. You make me feel wanted…" She crawled out of the tent. I held her hand, but she jerked it off.

"*Astaghfirullah*," she muttered, and started walking, five feet away.

"You only crib about the night."

"Fatima, I…I…"

"*Hmm*?" She said, without turning.

"Nothing!"

7

"Tell me a story, Abheer. I'm bored," Fatima said, walking beside me, a foot away, of course.

"Why not? Now that we are back to basics? The night," I chuckled.

"Shut up! We're walking only. You'll reach home soon."

"After walking *twelve* kilometres, yes!"

As we trudged down the road in the evening, noises from the marketplace meddled in our conversation. Some shops had electricity; yellow lanterns lit the others. All of them were flooded with people. As Fatima walked through the crowd, they did not budge, *again*. If they got to know Fatima's story, would they shun her just the same? Or would they just listen to it and forget the next day? If Fatima were a *kulakshani*, how could she shed that off when she walked out of Kainat? If she could, why did she still live there?

My thoughts burst at the seams; my teeth cluttered. I had closed my arms. I was shivering. Fatima had draped that cloth around herself, and we had not even stepped out of Assi Khurd yet.

"How versatile that cloth is!" I taunted.

"It's what?" She asked, caught unawares.

"It made your *hijab*, it made your floor, and now it's your shawl. And I am stuck here in this cold," I rolled my eyes.

"I am smart, yes," she chuckled.

"Yes, Ms. Smart. You laid that on the ground. You're washing your hair, and your dress now. *In this cold.*"

"Smartness does come for a price, Abheer," she said, and we laughed.

"Tell me a story, *na*! I am bored," Fatima frowned like a child.

"Who am I, by the way? *Panchtantra*?"

"*Bhak*! I don't know. Entertain me."

"*Arre!*"

"*Huh!*"

"*Achha* okay. Just one I happen to remember."

"*Yayy!*"

"A husband and a wife once entered into a bet—whoever opened the main door for anyone first would lose…"

"…the door to their heart?" She chuckled.

"*Eh*! Shut up! They locked themselves in their house."

"*Achha* okay!"

"That day, the man's parents visited them. They kept knocking at the door, but no one opened. They left…"

"*Haww!*"

I could not help giggling at that. "*Achha* I'll stay shut now," she said, placing her index finger on her lips. We burst into laughter.

"*Shhhhh!* Listen. So nobody opened the door, and his parents left. Two days later, though, the woman's parents showed up. The man knew they would have to go too—his wife…*tch*…could not lose. However, as the doorbell kept ringing, the woman started weeping. She lost the bet but didn't let her parents leave.

A year later, they had a son. Two years after that, they had another. The couple was as happy as they could be. Finally, a year and a half later, they had a daughter. But this time, the man threw a grand party.

Why didn't you do it for the boys, when the woman asked, he said, *because our daughter will open the door for us.*"

Fatima had a faint smile on her face. "Women are like that, Abheer," she said.

Beyond Assi Khurd, roads filled with chirping crickets, flickering yellow incandescent bulbs hanging from the walls of some huts and not the others, and

Fatima's silence. Stray dogs howled here and there, claiming the unmanned territory, perhaps. Fatima walked through the long trails of darkness with an unfaltering gait, as if the night could not eat us. I wished she had not dropped off her stick. I wished I could hold her hand.

"You would do that for your mother too. Losing the bet," I said, matching pace with her.

"*Oh!* I would lose *any* bet for her," she smiled.

"Fatima…"

"*Hmm?*"

"Why do you still live in Kainat?"

"Because it's my home. *Ammi* believes *Abbu* still lives there. *I* believe *Abbu* still lives there."

"No. How easily you can get away from your curse… *bleh*…bulshit. Just leave that village, why don't you?"

"*Huh!*" She sighed. "Look around Abheer," and I did.

A series of dilapidated huts, cobwebs at all the corners of the porch, on the pillars, the window mesh. These houses did not have incandescent bulbs, or *any* light; it was pitch dark. Unwanted ivy sprang out of pores on the walls; dirt had settled wherever it did not. I could have said no one lived there, but most hand-pumps had wet bases and clothes hung on some of the ropes.

"This is where," she said, "people from Assi Khurd who share my curse live." Sweat flushed all over my body.

"Why do they live in such darkness?"

"We are not allowed to light our houses, Abheer. They fear us, but they can always become a mob."

"Is that why…" I choked. *Is that why you wouldn't let me walk you home?*

"*Hmm?* Is that why?" She asked.

"Nothing. Fatima…what if…these people…they find out about you?"

"They'll kill me," she said, just casually, "and offer my body to their deity, apologize for the sin they have contracted, celebrate that they have mitigated it."

"Why don't you just run away. To somewhere far, where this thing doesn't follow you. Come to my city."

"Run *away*? *Huh! Ammi* won't go. *Abbu* lived here, died here."

"And you? What about you? How do you say she loves you then? Why do you believe that?"

At that, her head turned. Her eyes snarled, her teeth clenched. We walked in stark silence for good five minutes before she broke it.

"I didn't, until that evening," she said.

"What evening?"

"What do you think, Abheer, everyone believes in the curse?"

"I don't, Fatima. I think you are…"

"*Shhhhh…bhak*…shut up! Everyone does not believe in the curse. Some men don't, and they predate. Many girls, who they call *kulakshanis* otherwise, they rape when no one's watching. Tahira was raped when she was fifteen. She still shivers around men, Abheer."

"…and you people did nothing about it?"

"*Haha!*" She mocked. "We're *kulakshanis* Abheer. They fear us when alone and crush us when together. That's all."

"Aren't there boys who share your curse too? And other families?"

"Yes, there are, but what?"

"Why doesn't anyone help?"

"We are outcasts, Abheer. We hate our existence. How do we *ever* love other people?"

I swallowed a lump.

"That evening," she continued, "two years ago, I was returning from the woods. *Ammi* wanted some firewood. Just as I had entered the road to my hut, a hand pressed against my mouth. I knew what it was. As he dragged me, I prayed my muffled screams would reach *someone. Someone* would save me. His other hand was on my chest already.

Then his hands eased. They slid down; he collapsed. It was *Ammi*, with a wooden rod in hand."

"*Phew!*"

"Yes, *Ammi* saved me. But she didn't run away with me; she stayed. As he lay on the ground, passed out, she kept swinging her stick upon him—his stomach, crotch, head, full arc swings.

You killed Arkham. I won't let you touch my daughter.

Harami…my daughter. You would dare not look at…touch. You swine…

People had circled around us, a radius as long as their lives were distant from ours. Petrified, frozen, they watched *Ammi's* rage—the *kulakshani* had summoned the demon upon her mother. None of them budged. None of them stepped up to save the man. *Ammi* marred his face.

When *Ammi's* fit of rage was over, she clasped my wrist and walked me into our hut. She threw me onto the floor, clutched my scalp and slapped me left and right. Her eyes watered, her teeth locked—her solidarity was peeling off. Her sobs bit at me like a lion's fangs as she broke one broomstick after another on my back. As if with every swat, the love that dripped from her rage, her eyes, her quivering body would ooze out of my memory.

When she resigned from her beating, I couldn't move. She collapsed on the cot and stopped containing her sobs. And I lay there, my chest against the floor, assaulted, bruised…loved."

A savage silence mummified me. Her words wound upon my skin so tight they benumbed it. Places kept changing from populous, lively villages to precarious, unmanned fields. My vision blurred—Fatima turned into a silhouette I shambled after vacantly.

How do you take that about someone you love?

How could I tell Fatima she deserved love when the only time she had ever felt it, shards of broken glass had sniped at her from everywhere? How could I, when she had undressed her wounds in front of me every night? How could I, when I had picked that glass from her skin myself, one piece after another, one day at a time? How could I, when I had seen her blue, ruptured skin erupting like a volcano as the glass withdrew from it? How could I, when my fingers had laced with her blood?

How could I be her mirror when it was the glass she feared?

How could I, for whenever she looked at glass now, a lurid, blinding light reflected off it, made her cover her eyes, look away? I could whisper in her ears that she was beautiful, sacred, lovable, but would that ever suffice? And even if she braved through the glass, looked at my reflection of her, what then? How would she believe *I* was the clean mirror? How would she believe that her mother, her village—all who had ever shown her she was a *kulakshani*, were stained?

And if she believed me, would she walk the distance? Would she touch the mirror without fearing her touch would become the epicentre of cracks all over the glass? Would she trust that the glass would not disintegrate into shards this time, would not pierce her skin?

Would she trust that this time she would not bleed?

We walked through a pitch dark trail, but the place felt a bit less strange. I did not know where we were; I did not care.

"Fatima…"

"*Hmm?*"

"I love you…" I said. She froze. "I don't know how else to say this, Fatima. I…I love you…"

She turned, her eyelids dropping so she could only see my feet. "You're mad," she said in a faltering, spooked voice.

"No, Fatima, I'm not. Everyone else is, though. Why else would they treat you like a curse on their lives? With you, I have felt the happiest…and I know I cannot fulfil…but…but I love you. It's not…nothing…"

I must have been weeping too, for why else would she cry?

"Abheer…don't do…" I pressed her lips with my finger.

"I don't know Fatima…how to make you believe me…I just don't. Just know that I have never said this before…to *anyone*…know it, believe it. Please. I don't know what to say. I love you."

Her lips quivered beneath my finger; they brushed it wet. Her sniffs blew it cold.

"Abheer…I…"

"If this means anything to you, you'll not stop yourself, promise me."

"Promise…what," she asked.

"*Bhak!*"

Just then, someone jerked her away.

Slap! Another! Left! Right!

She did not stop slapping her until she was crying. We stood outside Fatima's house.

"*Ammi*, listen to me, I swear on Allah…"

"*Haramzaadi!*" She roared.

She gripped her arm and started dragging her. Fatima kept wailing, her gaze shuffling between her fuming mother and me. Maybe she loved me; maybe she did not. I did not want that moment to whizz past us like that, but it was slipping away.

And…the door slammed shut.

8

Maybe Fatima did not love me.

Why else would she not show up even in my last night in Kainat?

Yes, she *knew* that I was leaving.

A contemptuous silver crescent in the sky tore through the thin, low-lying fog. As I sat cross-legged on the itchy, dew-drenched grass, the darkness kept frittering away—it would be dawn soon. The mocking breeze must mess with my hair before it invaded my hoodie and froze me. Crickets warbled around me, scattered in the same grass I sat on. As bats glided in the air in circles, a part of their trajectory involved staring me in the eye and threatening to hit me head-on. Just when the challenge became rivalry, though, they took a sharp turn in front of my eyes and flew away.

The night laughed at me.

Maybe I was being hard on her; maybe she was stuck.

Maybe, or maybe not.

Ten days had passed since her *Ammi* had seen us together. Ten days of snooping at her from behind the rusty, dilapidated *thela* in her street every noon, when she dried and braided her hair in the sun, practised her *cleansing of the eyes*, squinted at the sky, laughed as she chatted with *Taiji*, even *Tahira* on some days. Ten days of hiding behind people, or standing cars or *samosa walas*, as I followed her on her evening errand to fetch firewood. Vigil always—no man should ever cast an eye on her. As she swung her carry bag in full circles, she hummed to songs that a few yards of distance rendered incoherent to me. Her gait—a mix of popping and long strides, no hint of missing someone. Every time she jumped from the earth, she landed on my chest and trampled my bones.

Maybe it was all Fatima's charade—*Ammi* must believe she did not think of me, of my *I love you*, anymore. Maybe she was dying to meet me, but the risk of giving that away to her mother followed her like a shadow. Her house had become more of a home now—you could hear *Ammi* shouting out to her to finish chores, and sometimes even giggles and laughter. On some afternoons, the mother-daughter duo sat in the sun outside, exchanging jittery words, nervous grins, awkward glances. *Ammi* was also confusing me.

Maybe Fatima did not know I was around; maybe she had not noticed me. Except that it was not true—we had exchanged glances the first day I had followed her. Maybe she cared about me; maybe not.

Ten days had passed, ten days of me sitting outside her house—my rump resting on pebbles, dust and rugged surfaces, my back stiff from unchanged posture, dozing off multiple times, waking in fear that I might have missed her. Ten days of me strolling in the fields every night. Ten days of me waiting for her to throw inklings in the air that she loved or missed me—none received.

"I bet you thought I wouldn't come," someone puffed on my earlobe. Fatima!

"*Aur kuch sochna chahiye?*" I screamed. My fist clenched; my eyes watered. My body flushed loads of sweat all over.

"I'll miss you, Abheer," she said with a puppy face. At that point, I could feel my chest burning. She sat down in front of me, but I turned my head away.

"Abheer!" She softened her tone.

"Abhee…"

"What do you think, Fatima? Just because I love you, and I told you…you…you could make me wait? Disapp…ear. You could…ignore…where were you? Didn't you want to talk to me? You knew I would be gone today right…"

"Abheer…I…"

"You what, Fatima? You knew I was everywhere around you, following you, but you chose to ignore me. Just because I love you, and you have the power to hurt me? Why did you make me wait, Fatima? Why? What if I had slacked? What if I was not waiting here, at this hour? What if…what if I had left just an hour ago? What then, you would not meet me?

Tell me now, *kuch aur sochna chahiye?*"

"I knew you would be here, Abheer," she said, her tone frantic now.

"Yes, and that's why it was okay for you to just disappear and leave me wondering, confused, guilty and what not? *Hai na?*"

"Abheer, I am really sorry. I can explain everything. I owe you that. But it's our last night…"

"So you realize it's our last night. What if I had not stayed this long? What if I had left an hour ago?"

"Abheer…" She shifted to face me, but I turned my head away again.

"Abheer…"

"Abheeerrrr…"

"Abheeeeer…"

"*Kyaaaaaaaa?*"

"It's our last night…"

"*Haan toh? Dikh gaya* how much you care."

"Why would you say that?" Fatima's voice ruptured into sobs. "Abheer, do you know who you've been to me? To me, you have been hope. Ask me what life becomes without it—I have lived like that for seventeen years. I didn't know I had so much to say, before you started listening to me. I told you everything—about my mother, my curse, my battles, triumphs, defeats, despair, happiness, everything. And you listened. I didn't know, but I was healing throughout.

I am sorry I hurt you. But you ask me if I care for you. Tell me, how do you ever not care about lemonade in a scorching desert, about candles in power cut nights, or freedom in a prison cell? Tell me, Abheer, how do you ever not care about being understood, valued, loved?"

I kept mum.

"Abheeerrrr…"

"*Hmm*…"

"If you want me to go, I will go…"

"Shut up! Just keep seated, here, *mere paas*,"

She complied. We sat in silence and watched the sky change colours.

"Will you say something?" She asked, after a long trail of silence. I shook my head.

"Abheer, I am sorry, *na*…"

"*Hmm.*"

I loved her.

"Abheer, do you think distance will tamper with our bond?"

"I don't want to think of that right now. It will make me sad. I don't want to feel sad, *anymore*."

"Haan *bas bas*! I said sorry," she said. We chuckled.

We went mum again, as bit by bit, the morning took over. Fatima and I yawned to the chirps of cuckoos, as the sky turned orange from the rising sun. The breeze was less cold now.

My last day in Kainat was over.

Fatima fidgeted to sit in front of me, her eyes staring at my face now.

"*Abhir, ana ahibuk. Ana ahibuk, Abhir ...*"

"What language is that?" I laughed, but she did not. She got up and started dusting herself. I followed her lead.

"*'atamanaa 'an 'aqul lak dhalika…Ana ahibuk, Abhir.* I hope you will find me."

"Find you where?"

"There…" she said, pointing up. "In the sky of a million stars." Except that it was morning now.

"I don't understand a word. What are you saying?"

"I must leave now, Abheer. It's morning."

"Oh yes, yes! But tell me first what you meant."

"Until then," she said, "keep my souvenir." Fatima planted a chaste kiss on my right cheek.

"*Astaghfirullah*," she said, almost in a whisper, before she turned and started walking away.

"Fatima…"

"I must go," she said, without turning.

"*Hmm.*"

I never saw Fatima after that.

9

Three Years Later

I have Fatima's letter.

I have loved her, you hear me? All through her absence—through the letters I wrote to her every second Sunday under my yellow study lamp, overwriting to bold: **109, H7, St. John's School of Liberal Arts, Mumbai**.

Through checking with the telephone *kaka* every night for an orange envelope, or a call, receiving none. Through the fading memory of her voice, her face. Through forgetting the touch of her calloused fingers, her extra canines, her laugh, vicinity, stories, the night— how she made me feel.

Through wondering how she must be. Through waiting out days, months, three years. Through attaching love to longing for her.

Through wondering if she missed me, if she received my letters, if she read them.

But today I return home after finishing college, enter my room and find this envelope in my drawer, dated three years ago. Have I ever felt happier? Mumma tells me it slipped from her memory. *Just casually.*

But I have her letter.

So I throw off a bath.

Don't have my rucksack.

Say no to shoes.

Leave my breakfast toppled.

Jump onto my clothes.

Change my bed…

…and tear open the envelope.

Dear Abheer,

Abhir, ana ahibuk…

Abheer, I love you.

I wish I had not hidden behind another language to tell you that, but I did. In many ways, I have failed you. But I swear I love you.

That night fell upon us like a wicked magician's trick, didn't it? You became the spectator—anxious about what must have happened to me. Me, the subject—shoved into a strange dimension, dark, unfamiliar, not knowing what existed around me, what the rules were. I do not even know if the metaphor makes sense.

That night, when Ammi threw me onto the bed, she did not hit me. I knew she was weeping—her back rubbed against mine.

She has been gentle ever since. Her words—less harsh. Her actions—less violent. She has been asking about you, although she never mentions that night. In some nights, she even woke me up. 'He must be waiting for you.' Maybe she feels she has caged me my whole life, that I must be desperate to break free.

Maybe it is true—she has caged me, except that this cage has become my home now. That is what we do, don't we? We get comfortable in sadness, pain, a distant idea of happiness. And when happiness becomes a real possibility, our universes start crumpling.

You see, Abheer, I could have accepted your love, but to what end? Allah would not accept you; Ammi would not accept you. Now, you will tell me we could flee from all of this. But flee? My village would laugh at Ammi. Leave Ammi to rot in that torment? Open my eyes to a beautiful life, believing everything was just a bad dream?

None of this is a dream. My curse is my reality; my Ammi is my reality.

As I write to you, Ammi is packing. She cannot stand this village anymore. Maybe there is hope that I can heal her. You see Abheer, you may have been a beautiful escape, but only this can be my redemption.

We are leaving to somewhere far off. My curse will not find me there; I hope you do—start looking from the roots. I wish we meet again. In a place far, far away, amidst people who do not know either of us, just by chance, I wish we do. I am going to wait for you.

I believe in Maktub—everything is written. If Allah wants us to meet, we will. Until then, if you ever wish to feel my presence, find me there…

In the sky of a million stars.

Love,

Fatima Hassan.

A Wistful Woman's Chronicle

1

Jaipur, Rajasthan. 10th June 2012. 10:00 P.M.

For once, she wanted to sit in silence and watch the world glow.

She sat at the edge. Her legs dangled down into the abyss, scratching against branches that grew off the vertical land. Her gaze—blurred, fixed on a city that sparkled. It was 10 P.M. The yellow, green, red, golden city lights glittered on a seemingly boundless blanket.

Mridula was fifteen when she was married to a fifty-six-year-old man in Mandwada Khalsa, a village near Pindwada district in Rajasthan. That village did not even exist on the map, so insignificant to the lovelorn man in a tuxedo sitting with a beer bottle to her left, to the Armenian man she had slept with just the previous week, or to that city beneath her feet. Yet, to her, it remained the origin of her indelible scars. The viewpoint was the most romantic spot in the city, they said. Beside her, a couple had just discovered the bliss of a French kiss. The sound of their lips separating plunged her into memories of her teenage love.

In symphony with a group of teenagers' music, memories filled her up.

I wish I could leave you my love but my heart is a mess.
My days they begin with your name and nights end with your breath.

"Prateek Kuhad is love," screamed one of them, raising her vodka bottle.

"Romance! Love…" Mridula sniffed.

Her fingers tapped to the song's beats as it picked an unorthodox offbeat rhythm. Mridula was no newbie to the intricacies of music. At twelve, the finesse with which she played the *kamaicha* startled her father. They called her Bela then.

Bela's father led a group of *Manganiyars*, a hereditary musical community that played for their patron royalty, Rajvendra Pratap Singh. Every evening at four, they would sit to do *riyaaz*. As the setting sun left orange trails for the moon to follow, the balmy air cracked her lips and desiccated her skin. Bedsheets made perfect seats against the sand, which the scorching day had left searing. Men wore turbans of cloth soaked in water overnight; women wore *ghaghra*, *kanchli* and *ghunghat*.

Little Bela loved playing with her father's group. She tapped on the strings with her fingers like a witch casting a complicated, enchanting spell. The maestro that she was, she oscillated the bow across the strings in perfect sync with the beats of the *kartal*. As the singers hit the highest notes their vocal cords could, the folklore transcended a boundless expanse of yellow.

Her love for music was not the only thing that drove her to the practices, though. There was a boy—the son of Girdhari *kaka*, her father's fast friend and co-leader of the group. He played the *dholak*. As Bela plucked her strings, her gaze would not deter from her bow on purpose. At her vision's periphery, she would find him pining for her eyes to lift. That little misery she inflicted upon him flushed her stomach with butterflies. Her face blossomed; a grin cracked through.

Whenever she thought of it, she sniffed in disgust. Mridula's life had lacunas where demons lived; the song poked them. *Romance is an enticing cover to a book that always ends on the most terrifying note*, she whispered into the abyss.

Mridula Vashisht, thirty-seven, was an oppressed woman. At fifteen, love had failed her. She was raped into marriage. At seventeen, she had found herself on an empty road in the middle of nowhere, ripped of her identity, of her only hope of a family.

Mridula Vashisht, thirty-seven, had sinned too. That night, she had picked herself up and set out on a spree to extract revenge from the universe. She had given empty love to men, looted them of more than just wealth, and left them in wrecks. *The way to a man's heart is through his pants*, she said.

Mridula Vashisht, thirty-seven, sat through that night with voices in her head, horror in her soul. Was she a sinful woman? Was everything she had done her character's manifestation or just a weak heart's response to the most terrible things a woman could face? Her past—still unavenged. Her conscience—stained and guilty. All of this because of two men.

Mridula Vashisht, thirty-seven, craved a clean slate. All she needed was to wipe off the two men her horrid past stemmed from. As the night aged, her plot unfolded miles away in Mandwada Khalsa.

So Mridula sat through the night, still and calm, closer to the answers she sought, to the redemption she deserved.

2

Sancoale, Goa. 13th June, 2012, 4:37A.M.

And yet, no one would stick with him.

As Rishi's favourite singer screamed in his ears to numb the silence of the place, he strolled in the streets of his 207.63 acres' residential campus, the beauty of which he loved to boast.

> *…And I know*
> *I may end up failing too.*
> *But I know*
> *you were just like me,*
> *with someone disappointed in you…*

At 13, Rishi had discovered Linkin Park. He lived with his parents in Indore then, and had a band in school. The fascination had been such that Rishi wanted to be a musician for life. In tenth standard, he had even done some permanent damage to his vocal cords, trying to do harsh vocals like Chester Bennington.

Then life swept him off, and music became a personal thing for him. New artists found places in his playlist alongside Linkin Park. Yet, when things fell apart, that would be the playlist he turned to—it reminded him of innocent years, simpler times.

His chest continued to ache from the last night's episode.

Maybe what we fear the most is a guilty conscience.

When you hurt someone, you scavenge for things they have wronged you with. You list everything you can and amplify the things you find, just so your conscience acquits you of the guilt. And you are afraid to go where these reasons shall be difficult to find. You are scared you will hurt them, and find no explanation for it. They will not even hurt you so the scores level.

Maybe that is why Sachi's crooked ex-boyfriend had had her heart, but Rishi could not.

Why else would Sachi tell Rishi he was the most genuine guy she had ever met, but deny his love when he came with it? Just the previous night he had proposed to her, and she had said her heart was still stuck.

He had cut the call to her face. She kept texting him *sorry*—she did not want him to wait for her. She knew he would hurt himself in that wait, which she could not see ending.

Rishi did not take her calls, and did not reply to her texts because:

1. He was hurting, and,

2. Something called the male ego is deeply, fundamentally rooted in all men. Rishi was no exception to that.

He had not slept the night. He might lose the emotional intimacy they shared. It had taken him a year and a half to open her that much; he could not start all over.

He must talk to her. She must let everything out—why her heart was stuck, the moments she cherished, the fears she housed, everything. She must speak about herself; she rarely ever did.

She did not hate her ex-boyfriend. She held on to the good memories and fought the scary ones every day. She did not hate him, though he had screamed at her for no fault of hers, abandoned her in the middle of the street, stopped taking her calls and seeing her texts. She did not hate him even though he blamed her for everything when *he* wanted to leave. She did not want him back, though.

She did not hate him because when it was the first time she had experienced love, it was for him. It was special. She hated scarring beautiful memories with the hurtful events that followed.

If her ex-boyfriend ever faced Rishi, he would not stop punching him until his eyes turned into swollen black bulbs, and his nose bled in fleshly pulps. She was the most important girl in his life. He wanted to give her all the love he could, but she did not take it. She dreaded attachments now.

Rishi understood all of this. Would she understand him just the same? Months ago, when they were just friends, she had promised him she would get out of her state. Yet, she had not. Now that she knew he loved her, would she?

He loved her. He fucking loved her. The rush of blood he felt whenever he made her laugh, he had never felt before. But she had detached herself from everyone. She did not get hurt now, but you could not touch her too. She did not trust people with her feelings anymore. She lived inside the protective walls of her own making, so closed she started to weep whenever she talked about herself.

The best people in the world deserved to be fought for. So Rishi would stay, stick around, break her shells if he might, love her with everything he had.

She was his happy place. He wished he would become hers someday.

Rishi's phone rang. *Papa* flashed. Grandma was on the phone, though.

"Rishi, take the next flight to Indore, take your mom, and come here," she said, barely hiding the panic in her voice.

"…but what happened?"

"Your *dadaji* is in hospital," she said. But the last he knew, he was fine. In fact, busy. He had some legal formality to look to regarding a piece of land he owned. Last week, his father had gone to Mandwada Khalsa for the same.

"What! How is he?"

"…come fast!"

"…how's papa?"

The line died.

3

**Mandwada Khalsa, Rajasthan.
15th June 2012. 4:07 A.M.**

Fragments of burning wood dripped from the pyre like molten lava. Fangs of the fire roared as they gnawed against the wind's fury. When the body had burnt just enough, the crematorium workers (*dom* by caste, as Rishi's *tauji* addressed them) cracked the skull with bamboos. The fire swallowed the brain's flesh—a tiny explosion within the pyre.

Rishi sat at a distance, his blurry eyes fixed at his grandfather turning to ash, minute by minute. Never before had he seen death so closely. Just yesterday, his grandpa lay on the floor in his mansion, wrapped in a saffron linen shroud, nostrils stuffed with cotton, buried beneath a heap of marigold garlands. Grandma sat at his feet, hallucinating grandpa beside her, gossiping about the dead body to him. Whenever the delusion broke, she would swing her arms at her chest and cry as if her fists held shards of broken glass. Rishi's mother and the other ladies held her back, sobbing themselves. His father stood frozen at a distance, staring vacantly at the dead figure.

As per Mandwada Khalsa's tradition, only the youngest male in the family could light the fire. At the *ghat,* Rishi's wet hair had fallen in crumbs as the barber shaved his head. So was done to his grandpa's corpse. When the barber accidentally made a cut on his head, there was no blood. No groan. No pain. No life.

As the sun marched to the top, the sky changed colours. The summer breeze was the only thing pleasant about the entire setting. Rishi's father still wore a blank look. Ever since Rishi could remember, his father had been a silent, inexpressive man, who only spoke when necessary, who never yelled unless at his mother. How could he ever have been the playful, lively boy from Grandma's stories? *But then, one day…*she would break off, always at this point in the story. Always!

"Some women are witches," she sighed.

Rishi despised her for it—for the accusations she hurled upon his mother just like that. The words, the taunts, everything. One summer he had seen her twisting his mother's arm, calling her *karamjali.* His mother had forgotten to turn off the gas knob in time. The milk had boiled out of the vessel. He was seven then.

Ever since then, he had never missed another clue— hiding the keys to the storeroom from her, blaming her for every little mismanagement, the clutched teeth, the jibes. Grandma did not like her. He had often been desperate to call her out, but his mother would not let him. "She is your *dadi*," she would assert, her eyes so wide open they almost popped out.

Rishi's father had neither wept a tear nor slept a wink. He wanted to talk to him, but when had fathers and sons ever been vulnerable? Rishi was not grieving, though. At least not as much as his father. Maybe because in the seventeen years of his existence, only summer holidays had had grandpa in them. Grandpa had been poisoned. Rumours had it that he had rushed to Pindwada to meet someone the previous day. *Not important*, he had said when grandma had asked. The look on his face—nervous and frantic.

At a far end sat a woman, doubled up against the tent that sold firewood, writing in her diary. Outsider, Rishi thought, for Mandwada Khalsa women would not breach the tradition—step foot in a cemetery. She must be in her early thirties. She wore *Ghaghara Choli*, embedded with ethnic mirror-work, beads and sequins of all colours, no *chunni*.

"Women shouldn't be present at the cemetery, though I don't believe in that. Who are you?" Rishi asked, walking up to her.

"How are you related to Rajvendra Pratap Singh," asked the woman in a flat voice, without caring to look up.

"I am his grandson," At that, her gaze lifted.

"Are you Ranvijay's son?"

"Yes, but how do you know? And who are you?"

The woman's eyes did not flutter. Her face froze with a mysterious, enchanted look, not giving Rishi any clue about what was happening. Brown eyes, sandalwood complexion, shoulder-length hair—she threw around a magnetic charm. Without wavering her gaze, she crumpled the page from her diary and threw it off. Then she held Rishi's hand, got up and walked off.

After she disappeared, he picked up the piece of paper.

Every fang of the flame that swallows him
renders one bone of me serene.
One root turned to dust; the other shall be soon—
will leave a slate fresh, a past clean.

Rishi stood there, puzzled, stressing on his brain to join the dots he could not even see.

4

Baga Beach, North Goa. 30th June 2012. 12:17 P.M.

The Goan summer sun reflected off cars crawling in lines on the road, like a colony of ants. The beach lay below him, sprinkled with people. From a thousand feet above the ground, everything looked insignificant.

As they descended, Rishi's gaze would not stop shuffling between the fabric wing above and the air column beneath, a thousand feet deep. Every time he looked down, his heart thumped. Buying this paragliding experience for two thousand rupees might just have been a bad idea, for

i. He feared height.

ii. He loved saving his pocket money.

iii. He did not have any lust, per say, for trying out new things. FOMO, YOLO were not his things really.

His life was haywire right now, and this new venture was more horror and less the respite he sought.

It was noon, midway between pleasant and hot. The seashore looked like a strip of silica separating a blanket of green from water that extended beyond the horizon. His stomach tickled, churned. Air friction? Anxiety? He did not know. The instructor poked at his waist—he must raise his legs to level with his butt.

Another paraglider flew past him. No instructor, just a woman. Or perhaps the woman was an instructor off duty. Rishi had seen her somewhere. At the cemetery? No way—she wore navy blue jeans shorts and a neon Adidas polo T-shirt, not *ghaghra chunni.*

They landed.

She was the finest figure of a woman—sandalwood complexion, eyes like popsicles, shoulder-length hair, body the shape of an hourglass. Her charm so magnetic, so familiar, it wrenched his gut. As they unfastened their belts, she put on her Ray-Ban shades.

"Have I seen you, somewhere?" Rishi asked. Although, he was sure by now—the cemetery woman.

"Nice beanie," she said, pointing at his black Adidas head gear. It was not so nice, though. It itched at his bald head.

"*Umm*…thank you?"

"You're acrophobic, right?" She said.

"How do you know? Did I look so restless?"

"*Haha!* No. I just pick little things."

"Okay! So what did you pick exactly?"

"You were looking up to check the fabric wing every now and then, and every unusual stir made you uncomfortable." She said.

On point, but why were you observing me so closely? Rishi thought.

"*Hmmm.* Okay. Nice…"

"Also, you are depressed," she said, nudging him with her elbow, smiling as if they were friends. They walked on the sand. Waves kissed their feet.

"I am not depressed. I am just a little…sad. Actually, things have been a little rough lately. But…Hi, I am Rishi, by the way," he said, shaking hands with her.

"And you?" He asked, when she did not introduce herself. She still did not bother to speak.

"You were good, by the way," Rishi said with a sly smile.

"I mean, you were flying all alone, without an instructor. And not restless or budging at all, you were good."

"…okay. How good exactly, tell me?"

"Just as good as you are hot…" he said, winking. He liked to believe he could flirt. She chuckled.

"*Uff!* Hot like this coffee?" She said, prodding at a shaker she pulled out of her handbag.

"How hot is it, tell me?" He said with that same sly smile.

"Just as hot as you."

"*Ooof!* Beware, your hand might burn." They laughed.

RULE I: Always give a man gratification. Feed his ego.

"We'll keep your story for the next conversation." She winked, sipping from her shaker.

"What story?" He asked.

"You want to be listened to, Rishi. I know," she nodded.

RULE II: Understand them, and say it out loud. Show interest, and intent.

As they walked in silence, beach noises filled in. A man's screams tore through the grunt of crashing waves as he lashed out at his jet ski bike instructor—he should have told him the surges could topple him over. A young woman in a white tank top and denim shorts giggled in her lover's arms as he held her around her waist, swept her off the ground, and kissed her on the neck. A little boy's friends shouted to him to run with them on the water, but he would not budge from the perfect dome he had shaped on his sandcastle.

"Have I seen you somewhere," he asked again.

"Should you wish to fly again, call me," she said. She handed him her visiting card; her smile transitioned into a customary one.

Mridula Vashisht

Zen Adventures

Was all of this a bait? No, it felt so genuine.

RULE III: Pull back. Puncture their ego. He will come chasing.

Rishi could not afford to feel any more cynical at this point—there was a void in his chest. As Mridula walked away, loneliness, like water that breaks past a dam, gushed in.

5

Sancoale, Goa, 1ˢᵗ July 2012. 11:39 P.M.

As he squeezed his eyelids with a finger and thumb, tears oozed out. Rishi yawned in his desk.

A multicolour hand-painted Jodhpuri photo frame lay on his desk. Right beneath his LED study lamp, dimmed to the lowest, neck adjusted away from his eyes. Memorabilia from their Jodhpur trip. He had bought that frame from a flea shop for as cheap as forty-seven rupees. Summer vacations, 2005—the only time his father had decided to take them on a trip without him pleading. He had had a row with grandpa the previous day.

The frame housed a picture of his parents—his father, Ranvijay Pratap Singh, and his mother, Sugna Singh. He had begged them both to pose. Mehrangarh Fort in the background. His father's arm around his mother's shoulder—they must look like a couple. Yet, their sides did not touch. Their teeth tore through their lips for forced, customary smiles.

As his fingers interlocked upon the desk, his chin rested on the thumbs. His weary, watery eyes would not deter from the photograph. Of course, he reminisced— that was the least dysfunctional his family had ever seemed.

By five, Rishi had learnt that his father did not love his mother. By six, he knew how much his mother yearned for it.

At seven, he had asked her, "Papa doesn't love you *na, maa?*"

A sobbing Sugna had covered his mouth with a quivering palm. Shoving his face in her chest, she had said, "He is your father, *beta*. You should not talk like that."

So Rishi never talked like that. He became the shy, obedient son who never questioned his silent, taciturn father. When they spoke to each other through him, he mediated with resignation. When his father would not even care to turn to his mother when she spoke, when he said nothing and absolutely nothing. As the silence made her weep, he would walk past. When he raised his voice at her, he would clench his teeth but say nothing.

When she retaliated, though, with the same jibes, the same silent treatment, the same hushed, angry words, he walked up to her.

"Why do you do this, *maa*? You know it won't make any difference. You're trying to melt an iceberg with a lighter," he would say to his weeping mother, for it truly never made any difference. She would throw explicit declarations in the air that she was angry. For days, Rishi would have to serve him dinner, make his bed at night, and sometimes even dye his hair. But Ranvijay never budged. At last, Sugna resigned, and things went back to normal.

If only it stopped there! If only his father did not abandon her when grandma attacked! If only he said something when she accused his mother of nonsensical things! She called her *karamjali* as if it were her pet name. Many a time, she even abused her dead father. If only he did not leave her weeping! If only he did not resort to his usual silence, as grandma hurled false accusations and melodrama at her when she retaliated!

Grandma had long fallen from grace in Rishi's eyes. Grandpa, and to some extent, his father too. All of them.

Rishi's grandfather, Rajvendra Pratap Singh, was one of the Rajput royalties in Rajasthan. The most revered man in Mandwada Khalsa, he had served as the Sarpanch for five full tenures, had fallen five months short of the sixth. Besides being the wealthiest in the village, or the whole Pindwada district, he had also been the most influential, resourceful and benevolent man. His mansion functioned as a king's court; his living room couch a throne. The villagers called him *Deewan Sahab,* and his words never ranked any less than judicial orders.

Rishi's favourite childhood memory with his grandpa was sitting beside him on his sofa in such sessions. *Chhote Deewan Sahab*, they called him. He boasted of his grandfather's legacy to all his friends. Grandpa told him stories of Rajasthan's heritage, their valour and pride, how their women were their honour, how they must be veiled. Any infringement upon that should mean, and had meant in the past, war.

Rishi had always been the pampered grandchild. As a single child, he was their *khaandan ka chirag*. As a kid, he liked his grandma. She stocked mangoes for him every summer. She also bought *dalmot* (a dry snack) from a local vendor he particularly liked. She turned Rishi's every wish into everyone's command, always.

He scrolled through his phone, tapped on *Maa*, but hung up before the first ring. Outside his window stood a three-storey under-construction apartment, with steel railed balconies and windows with wooden frames painted white. Before that building had happened, his room stayed sunlit till five-six in the evening. To its left hung the moon in solace, a thick crescent in that starless night.

Rishi missed the mundane normality of his family. Dysfunctional could feel normal, right? At least no one had poisoned his grandfather, and his father was not in shock? At least he did not go without a bath for days or shower for hours when he did? At least he did not sit in the dark and plead not to be disturbed? At least his mother did not weep on the phone every day. At least everything was not falling apart?

Rishi tapped on the lamp. Darkness fell. The moonlight became significant, and his thoughts shifted to his newly failed love adventure.

As he stood up, he jerked the chair so hard it toppled. He let himself fall upon the bed, a free fall against the chest. Tired as he was, he would fight his thoughts till sleep got him.

6

Baga Paralia, Baga Beach, Goa.
2ⁿᵈ July 2012. 12:00 A.M.

"Tell me something?" Mridula asked.

"Hmm?"

"Why that beanie? You were wearing it that day too."

"I am bald right now, ma'am."

"It does not go with your shirt, that's all," she said. He wore a maroon half-shirt with local print.

"Madam, meeting you was an impromptu decision. I didn't dress for it," he rolled his eyes playfully.

"Huh! I knew you would call," Mridula said.

"Ahha! So much information to process. How is your headspace keeping?" Rishi retorted

"I have a flair for reading minds, you see. I am pretty good at it." A flirtatious smirk flared on her lips as she sipped from her *Virgin Mojito.*

"*Uff!* Interesting!" He waved his palm at himself like a fan and rolled his eyes, dismissing her acclaim. They laughed.

"My powers are interesting indeed," she raised her brows.

"Your extra-curricular activities definitely are. Seldom do I see lady paragliders. And mind you! I live in Goa."

"*Haha!* Thank you," she blinked to accept his compliment.

Mridula had once slept with a wealthy American businessman who wanted to love her. He had bought her many luxuries and experiences. Adventure sports had been one of them.

A few years back, Mridula worked as a housekeeper at a hotel in London. Being a five-star hotel in the city, it attracted the richest and the most influential people. From lavish stays to whims and fancies, the hotel catered to everything. Everything.

So some housekeepers did more than changing bedsheets and towels. If you sought it, they would find you. Eyes that flirted, irresistible smirks, and a glossy, delicious cleavage. They would run their fingers upon your forearm, the ticklish imprint—their aphrodisiac of choice. Their scent complemented their mind compulsion just fine. All you had to do was buy them a drink, a specific drink—*sangria.* They would be yours for the night.

For usual guests, their services had charges; for the elites and the VIPs—complementary. For everything they earned, the manager kept a cut. Mridula was his favourite employee that way; she could slay with her eyes.

Of hundreds she had slept with there, Mridula remembered that American businessman just fine—he had started with a kiss. The tickles of his fingertips grazing upon her back, his mushy kiss between her breasts, the shivers of his touch, the womanly instinct he managed to arouse. He believed in love the way kids believe in superheroes. He talked of trust, respect and hope as if they were not the children of wishful thinking.

Of all men, these were the most difficult kind to hurt.

Mridula Vashisht could shut that guilt off like a switch, though. She made him believe she loved him and fled with him to the U.S. She went to the fanciest restaurants and the most elite parties, met the most powerful people in America and made several influential friends. With his money, she bought herself a fancy farmhouse in Paris, taking good care that he could not trace it. All of this under the garb of love.

The day they were to marry, he woke up to pillows beside him, wrapped in her quilt.

It was midnight, but as it is with Goa, the night was still young. There was dancing. There was music and people in the trance of their lives. Restaurants had setups for candlelight dinner—umbrellas, candles in glass cases, plastic chairs or sofas, pink, red or orange mood lightings.

Near the sea, youngsters played Frisbee. Couples strolled on the wet sand holding hands. Some kissed.

Mridula blinked, nodded, and clasped his hand as Rishi vented about his grandfather's death. When he talked of his father, his numbness and the titbits of his family dynamics, she hugged him.

But why was Rishi telling her all of that?

RULE IV: Always listen. It seldom happens to men.

"So, what are your hobbies," Rishi asked, and they both laughed. They left the restaurant to walk in the open.

"Yeah, yeah, okay…okay. Don't laugh so much. I didn't know how to fill the silence."

"Small talk?" She raised her brows. "Really? You expect that of me now?" She continued to laugh.

"Stop, please. Hey…"

"Yeah, okay. So I'll answer your question. I like to write. I write poetry."

"What? Really?"

"Yeah, why? Don't I look like a poet?"

"*Ah!* Ma'am, you look like one fine poem."

"*Uff!*" She laughed again.

"What? It landed just fine. *Huh!*"

"It did. It did," she said, laughing still.

"May I have the honour of listening to something from you, madam?" He said when her laughter died.

"If you pledge never to speak like that again, yeah, you may."

He shrugged at that as she pulled out a diary from her handbag. *A Wistful Woman's Chronicle*, read the scribbling on its hardcover.

She opened the diary at the page with the ribbon and read:

You have built your walls with bricks of hate.
I am afraid; your castle might get blown away.
You burnt me in the flames of your wrath.
Would that your walls could stand the gusts of
my love.

I am afraid; I might love you to pieces.

I am afraid you will lie there, weak.
I am afraid you will cry.
I am afraid I shall be the reason why.
You may have forged yours with flames of hate,
but love melts hearts in mysterious ways.

I am afraid; I might love you...to pieces.

"Hey, you write well."

"Thank you." She said. Silence!

"*Ah*...can I call you Mrids, because Mridula is kind of long and heavy?" he asked. Mridula grinned.

"Okay. And what do I call you then? Rish…" He chuckled at that.

"No. Rishi is my shortened name only. My full name is Rishab Pratap Singh."

"Long and heavy!" Mridula mewled. They laughed.

"Yeah. Yeah. What's your story, Mridula? Did you fall in love?"

"Yes, when I was fifteen. Where we lived, we were not allowed to, but he had promised me a better world. So we eloped."

"*Ah*…I don't understand. You have said hate in your poem. Why did he hate you?"

"I was young, just like you. I believed it was hate, but it was not."

Rishi did not like being called young, but her story got the better of him.

"There is something stronger than hate—indifference. For once, love can shake hate, howsoever deeply rooted it may be. Indifference though! I am not so sure about that."

"What happened next?" Rishi asked.

He sold me to your grandfather for money. She did not say that.

"He got bored of me, so he accused me of things. None made sense. In the middle of a street, in a village all new to me. He kept screaming at me. I wept. Then he left and never came back."

His teeth gritted, jaw clenched. Rishi fumed. A personal story, Mridula could tell.

"People don't realize the scars they leave behind," he said.

"*Hmmm*," she buzzed.

"I love a girl, Mridula. Someone hurt her, too, the same way as you, in the middle of a street. I want to give her all the love I am capable of, but she does not take it. I want to punch that guy in the face…"

"…Breathe, young man." A long inhale. "Tell me more," she said.

"No. Some other time. We'll keep this story for our next conversation, Mrids," he winked.

Of course, that was cringe—it irked Rishi. Both the wink and *Mrids*.

"*Mridula* is just fine, I guess," he covered. She blinked in consent.

"This is queer, though," he said.

"What?"

"This. Me ranting about my life to you. I mean, I am seeing you for just the second time. You likewise."

"*Hmmm*."

"Queer, but nice. Warm and nice."

"What are we, Mridula? Friends?"

"Yes, of course," she said.

A few yards away, a woman lulled a four-five-year-old boy to sleep. As his cheeks pressed against her shoulder, she tapped on his head. Even her lip movements were incoherent. She must be singing *Chanda hai tu*, or *Pariyon ka desh*—Mridula knew only two lullabies. Her gaze kept oscillating between them as Rishi continued to speak.

"Rishi?"

"Yes?"

"What would you do if you were me and ran into my lover?"

"I would just kill him," he said, crushing his teeth.

"Exactly!"

7

Sancoale, Goa. 4th July 2012. 9:37 P.M.

"Are you back in your hostel," Rishi's mother asked over the phone.

"Yes, *maa*," he replied.

"Had a good time?"

"Yes!"

"Good! Now no more of these outings. Get back to studies from tomorrow. You know about papa *na*; how much faith he has in you? Don't let him down, *beta*," she said.

She always did that. Don't rent a scooty for trips—papa fears accidents. Don't do all-nighters with friends—papa does not want you to miss classes. Stop fishing for a life in the corporate world—papa wishes a better life for you. Study hard *beta*—papa has high hopes from you. When it was she who attached greater hope to him, she who always wanted him to excel. Who else did she have, except for him?

Inside Rishi's mother lived an abandoned woman who could not believe she could be loved. So she latched herself to Rishi, to her husband who did not love her, to a family that was outright dysfunctional. What else, if not that, could give meaning to her life? To Rishi, she always mentioned papa's expectations because hers would not weigh as much, she believed.

Except that it was not true. Rishi loved her.

"Yes, *maa*. I will."

"Rishi?"

"Yes, *maa*?"

"You have not been up to something, *na*?"

"Something, what?"

"You have not…drunk or anything *na*?" Rishi started laughing. His mother was often cute.

"No, *maa*. I have not done anything like that."

"*Beta*, you have made a promise to me. You remember that, *na*?"

"Yes, *maa*. Believe me."

"Repeat the promise you had made to me." She was too often melodramatic too.

"*Uff! Maa*. I have not drunk."

"Repeat!"

"Okay! Fine. I will never drink or smoke, and I will treat my wife with utmost respect and love…"

"Good, *beta.*"

"…unlike papa."

"*Hmmm.*"

"*Maa*, I will not drink, but you should not think of people who drink as bad people. This metric does not make sense."

"You are talking like this. Now I am scared."

"*Maaaaaa!*"

"Okay goodnight."

"Night."

Tired of the emptiness in his chest, he collapsed on his bed. A day on the beach with friends, to say. He had listened to the roaring waves better than any gossip his friends had had.

His phone buzzed beside him. *Sachi* flashed. He watched the call die, after which he texted her.

Rishi: Sorry, Sachi. I could not see your call in time. I have exams next week.

Sachi: It's okay. All the best.

Rishi: How have you been?

Sachi: I am okay, you say.

Rishi: A little less than okay.

Sachi: Hmmm.

Rishi: Was a call such a big thing, Sachi?

Sachi: I am sorry. I had health issues. Couldn't call at night.

Sachi: I did not want to bother you.

Rishi: Nice assumptions!

Sachi: Hmmm.

Rishi: It was not a big thing for you, na?

Sachi: What are you talking about?

Rishi: That I fell in love with you? It was not a big thing for you.

Sachi: No, Rishi. Why do you say that?

Sachi: I never wanted to hurt you, Rishi. It hurts me every day, but I am a heartless person. You'll hurt yourself, and I don't want that.

Sachi: You are a very nice person, and I don't deserve good people around me. I am a heartless person.

Rishi: Can you call me right now?

Sachi: Yes, wait.

How could she talk shit about herself? Just how? He loved her.

A dog-lover Sachi holding a white Bolognese to her chest, flashed on his phone. His favourite picture of her—she wore a black sweater. He picked this time.

"May I know why you're a heartless person or don't deserve good people around you?"

"I just am. Everything is not supposed to have a reason."

"I have asked you a million times not to bullshit about yourself, but if you still choose to do so, you had better have a reason, Sachi."

"I didn't call you for so many days and did not…"

"That's because you always crumble under the weight of such conversations. What else? Give me reasons?"

At that, Sachi burst into tears. Rishi shivered on the other side of the phone.

"Sachi, don't ever say such things about yourself."

"I am sorry!"

"I love you," Rishi said.

"I have hurt you, Rishi."

"I have been thoroughly hurt, but it is because of this entire setting, not you."

"Don't lie."

"I swear on Linkin Park."

"Chester is dead already."

"*Ouch!* Don't remind me of that." He giggled. She did, too, wiping off her tears.

"Sachi, I want to be happy, and I want to be with you. You are in a terrible state, and I want you to get out of it. I wanted that even when you were just a friend."

"I know. I will, with time."

"It has been a year and a half now. You are still stuck at your previous relationship. It is time you started healing yourself."

"I know."

"Sachi, I love you. And I want to believe that if someone can leave and scar the idea of love for you, someone can just stay and fix you too."

"*Hmmm.*"

Sachi had not called him ever since he had asked her out; he was angry. And that anger spilt in taunts here and there. Sachi surrendered herself guilty as charged.

"…And you should watch less of Bollywood, by the way," He said.

"What?"

"I am a heartless person," he mewled, then laughed. "Really, are you Sachi?"

"Stop with that." They laughed.

Both of them had missed talking to each other. An hour passed, then another, and another. It was 3 A.M. now.

"Sachi, you are on your meds, right? You should sleep."

"Yeah! Okay. Goodnight."

"Good Morning," Rishi said. She giggled. He hung up.

Rishi's heart sank.

8

Cavelossem, South Goa. 4th July 2012. 4:37 P.M.

As his hand fished for her bra strap along the trough of her spine, she rolled him over. Her tongue mushed his lips to distract him; her teeth bit them so hard they bled.

Mridula was on top of him now, wearing just her bra, perfumed like an Indian goddess. Soaked in *khus*, her hair smelt of an erotic communion of sunbaked earth and fresh rain. Her neck, so innocent, reeked of jasmine. Below that, harder fragrances followed. At the crux was her navel, perfumed with musk, as if it were the rendezvous for his lips, everything else a trail to follow. And as she opened her arms beneath him, an array of perfumed oils and powders blew him to ecstasy.

As a kid, Bela had seen her mother yearning for things to adorn herself with—sarees, jewelry, perfumes his father could never buy.

"Will I get to wear these someday, *maa*?" An eight-year-old Bela would ask her mother.

"You will, *beta*, when your time comes. But don't be a fool like me."

Her time had come.

I must tell you things about Mridula—

i. She could do disastrous things to men and feel nothing.

ii. Her eyes were one big catastrophe.

iii. She liked to have sex.

So there she was, in a house that barely qualified as not being a shack, having sex with a bartender. Only that this time, she felt as though she were making love.

She had seen him first at **Dom's Beach Shack**, a restaurant in Cavelossem. She was having dinner, and her eyes had fallen upon the man serving drinks at the bar. A few compulsive blinks, tension lines on her forehead, a stressed glance across the restaurant—it was him.

The fork slipped from her fingers. A chill ran down her spine. Her forehead flushed with cold sweat. As she lifted her glass of champagne to take a sip from it, it slipped from her shivering, panicky hands. Since there was no other waiter nearby, he approached her table to look to that. The champagne flooded the polished wooden floor, narrowing as it neared his approaching footsteps. As it kissed the tip of his shoes, he left wet trails behind him.

He had aged, and unlike Ms. Mridula Vashisht, not everyone aged like wine. Dark complexion, five feet and seven to eight inches tall (almost Mridula's height), wrinkled skin, wore a beach shirt, shorts and foam clog shoes. He must be forty but looked no less than fifty-five.

Twenty-two years had passed.

Her mind plunged her deep into memories of a time when love felt real. Bela's father often hosted dinners for Girdhari *kaka's* family. Bela helped her mother lay cots in the open for men to dine. In the kitchen, she wanted her chapattis to be so perfectly round that she pressed sharp lids over them. When they had arrived, she pressed her face against the bars of the window as her eyes refused to blink away from his notorious charm.

Men had dinner. *Kaki* and her mother sat beside them and gossiped. As Bela served chapattis, she would pray silently for her mother's boasting tendencies to show up, so he knew she had been the cook. Of course, it did not happen most of the time. Whenever it did, though, she stole her gaze from everyone and walked into the house with her empty plate and a smiling face.

One afternoon Bela sat outside her house, playing her *kamaicha,* when he appeared before her with a bundle of turbans. A blink away from the strings—it pounced from tension and pricked her thumb.

"Is *kaka* inside?"

"Yes," Bela said, sucking on her bleeding finger, quivering from the depth in his newly-cracked voice. He walked into the house.

Bela fetched a new string for her instrument. With a finger that would not stop bleeding, she plucked the broken string, groaning at every jerk. With a few more jerks, the bleeding severed. She stopped trying, lest she should stain the instrument.

"I will do it for you," a voice said from behind. Bela laid the instrument on the ground and stepped aside without saying anything. He plucked the broken string, fixed the new one, and wound the knobs to tighten it to the required frequency.

"Done!"

"*Shukriya*," Bela said, shying away.

"I am Nandkishor," he said. Bela got so intimidated she pressed both her fists against her back and would not lift her gaze from the ground.

"Tell me your name at least," he said, wearing his typical notorious smile. A moment's silence followed before Bela gathered enough courage to end it.

"I am Bela."

"Is your finger all right?"

"*Hmmm*," she nodded.

"Will you play stapoo with me?"

"Boys don't play stapoo," she said, now giggling.

"They don't, but I want to play with you."

"*Ummmm…*"

"Five in the evening, Barkha's backyard. I will see you there." He did not wait for a reply.

At five that evening, they had their first stapoo match. And that marked the beginning of Mridula's horrific love story.

He was a skinny man now. Years of drinking habit told upon his body—his hands shivered, dark circles beneath his eyes, constant reeking of alcohol. Amidst all her rage for him, a little pity was sprouting too.

When she had seen him last, she had had her first kiss, in a night in a village she had never been to before. He had promised to take her off to a city far away—a lived-happily-ever-after. When dawn broke, they would catch a ferry and leave Rajasthan.

He was not there the following day, though. She woke up in a moving jeep, mouth taped, hands tied to the back. She could not even scream, wail, or weep.

As he stooped down to pick the shards of broken glass, Mridula's long-dormant disgust started brewing. No man should ever make her shiver, shy away, panic. Especially not him. He had seen her with his side-glance. Had he forgotten her, or had he just ignored? Mridula was fuming.

The cold sweat, the panic, the shiver—everything vanished as if she could switch it off. Her destructive calm took over. She walked to him the way she had walked to every man she had ever gotten to bed—with poise, a seductive, pendulating gait, and her characteristic half-smile.

Five days later, she was in bed with him.

The bed shook as violently as it creaked. As he pushed inside her, as hard as a forty-year-old alcoholic body could, she moaned. Not because he pleasured her—how could he ever satisfy her like the younger boys, or the fitter, gym-built men she had slept with? Yet, she moaned as if it were her zenith.

RULE V: Always moan. Let them know they satisfy you. Hooks them.

He lay over her—missionary position. She hated lying under a man, feeling his racing heart thump against her breasts. She tried toppling him over, but he pushed her down. Why was she complying, losing control?

Mridula's universe started crumpling inside her. As he fucked her, she watched, with blurry, teary eyes, the fan's axle shake as it rotated. When he was done, he pulled out. It was pouring outside, but that was not the only reason she felt cold, even after sex.

The younger, gullible Bela, who was in love and vulnerable to him, was taking over. Twenty-two years later, he lay beside her, naked, both of them under the same blanket—Bela's *forever*, was it not?

He liked to lead, always. She followed, without questions. He had brought her to bed; she had let him. No hint of remorse in his eyes, no sign of repentance. He knew it was her, yet he should play a stranger.

That is the thing about a wounded heart. It expects the apology it deserves.

A wronged heart hurts, bleeds. That pain demands answers. You do not throw them out of your life, do you? You let them stay, keep them close, so they see the wreck they have made of you. You show them if they do not, sometimes shove it in their face. You want realization, acceptance, and a plea for forgiveness because only that shall be fair. A wounded heart resents.

A wounded heart expects things to be fair. And when that does not happen, it breaks.

He sprawled beside her for a while before he pulled the blanket off her chest. As he jerked her bra off, the blissful, delicious fragrance of her breasts hit him like a high. He started sucking on her left breast, fondling and squeezing the right.

The room was dull—ventilators stuffed with thermocol, closed, dusty windows, cobwebs at the corners, damp and smelly as if sunlight had not entered for years. Her eyes fell upon a *gudda* (a stuffed toy) lying at the top of his Almira, wrapped in thick dust.

Bela had had a *gudda* (Nandkishor) and a *gudiya* (Bela). She believed they were the manifestation of their love—

they must never separate. The night they were to flee, she had kept them in his bag.

"You lost the *gudiya*?" She asked. He swallowed a lump.

"It got misplaced when I shifted to this place." He said.

"You didn't care to find it?" A tear trickled down the corner of her eye as he kept mum.

"You…sold me."

For the first time in so many years, she wept. He would not even look at her.

For the next five minutes, her unkempt, subdued anger kept erupting like lava. As she whacked at him with her fists, she screamed. She cried at the top of her lungs, hurling accusations at him, demanding explanations, accepting none he gave.

A thing about women—when they love you, they love hard. When you hurt them, they do not give up. They look for silver linings in you until they exhaust every ounce of themselves. They get vexed in the process, though.

A vexed woman is…dangerous.

"I am sorry. I have wronged you. I am not a good man, Bela. I loved you, but my love was weak. It could be bought.

I took the money and fled to Goa, married a hippie I fell in love with and had two boys. Five years later, my family became dysfunctional. My wife and I parted ways. She took my kids along, and I became a drunkard. I am a lonely man, Bela. This loneliness perhaps is my atonement. I deserve this because I know I will never change," he sighed.

"You remember the love letters you wrote to me? I used to fall for them," she said.

The next she knew, he was coughing blood.

Mridula had saved her breasts for the last. Her imperfectly round, bouncy, impeccable breasts, fluffy and milky white, perfumed with saffron and white clove oil to drive him crazy, laced with poison.

She deserved revenge.

RULE VI: Hit them right when their pleasure has peaked.

She held him under the neck and pulled him up—the cough stained her arms, belly and breasts. "The letters you wrote to me, I fell for each of them. I know how empty words can be," she said, looking straight into his dying eyes. When the body had stopped shivering, she let it fall.

There she lay, naked, blood on her hands, her childhood love beside her…dead.

9

Dona Paula, Goa. 7ᵗʰ July 2012. 8:17 P.M.

"So, not a beach this time, *haan?*" Mridula asked, breathing in deep. The breeze was magical.

"*Ahha!*" Rishi exclaimed. "It's less crowded; you can even hear the wind. I get to hear you without the waves, bursting speakers or douchebags meddling. Isn't it better?" He grinned. As his elbows pressed hard upon the cemented railing, his reflection floated on the still water beneath. His legs intertwined like the loose ends of a string behind.

Mridula stood beside him, one hand on the railing, a vodka martini in the other. As she looked at Rishi with an unwavering gaze, the moon reflected off her watery, brown eyes; it was a starless night otherwise. The corner of her lips lifted just a little. Mind you, not too much, and mindlessly. Not a grin. Rishi was not telling a funny story. Just a little—she was a free, liberated woman now. She had detached herself from her past, and the suffering was now leaving her. In that moment, she was fully present inside her body, conscious of every dying trauma, as if they were things with shape and colour.

The touch of her rapist—brownish maroon amoebic patches on her skin, starting from her cheeks, down to her neck, her breasts, upon her arms, her thighs, all over her back. As the skin beneath them healed, the patches changed colour. The brown blended into the maroon, which then transitioned into red. At red, the patches melted into blood and dripped off. The newly formed skin surfaced, with marks that Mridula was sure would fade with time.

The treachery and emptiness from her failed love—a dull red, desiccated heart, not the biological shape but the shape of heart balloons. It dangled beneath her beating heart, joined to it by a thin piece of skin. As the emptiness left her, the heart shrunk and shrunk and shrunk. At the size of a candy, it burst.

"Mridula…"

She had done it to herself, hadn't she? She had picked herself out of the dark place she had been in for years. How was she anything less than a queen?

"Mridula? Mridula…"

Yet, there was a hole in the middle of her chest, a big black hole—the guilt of all her wrongdoings. It had a gravity so strong it pulled every organ of her body. Her insides still could not unclench. Mridula could not tell if the hole was shrinking already, but she knew it would with self-forgiveness. She was certain the hole would be dead soon.

Anyway, she was a queen. The lemon yellow sleeveless long-frock she wore, with dark green mini-checks, cut short to knee length with nothing less than a designer's finesse, was her royal robe. The tiara that adorned her braided hair—her crown.

"Mridula!" Rishi said, clasping her arm this time.

"*Ah!* Yeah…yeah?" She had zoned out.

"Why are you smiling?"

"*Ah!* Nothing."

"*Umm*…okay!" Awkward smiles followed.

"You've got a story to tell me," she said to Rishi.

"*Hmm*," he sighed. "Love is cliché. Rejections happen to everybody. Chuck it!"

"I am listening."

"I am listening," she stressed.

"There is this girl. We were in the same tuition in high school, but we started talking only after my secondary school got over. We weren't even in the same school. I just remembered her from high school tuitions, until I found her on the internet."

"*Hmm*. Go ahead."

"I was in my drop year—a lot of pressure. I would text her at night, and we would talk about hobbies, music, about *Harry Potter* and *The Fault in Our Stars* quotes. Conversations can soak your frustration like sponges, I learnt.

Our first phone call had lasted an hour and a half without either of us realizing. She would call me up at 1 A.M. at night, just like that. I would shut my laptop and free myself for the next two hours.

She resonates so much with my introvert self. When I get upset, it matters to her. She remembers all the little things I tell her. Every time I achieve something, she celebrates with me. She is an introverted, closed girl who seldom talks about herself, but she opens up to me. When she talks about the times she was hurt, I swear I feel like hugging her so tight nothing will ever touch her. Things like these…and a thousand other things.

I think it happened bit by bit, every day, over the expanse of a year and a half. The more I got to know her, the more I kept falling for her…"

"Old-School love," Mridula sighed.

"…but when such people get hurt, they build walls around themselves. She was mistreated in her relationship, in the exact same way as you…" At that, Mridula's conscience pinched her—she had lied.

"…She is still stuck there. I want to break those walls and touch her heart, but…"

"…you can only fix someone who wants to get fixed," Mridula completed.

"*Hmmm.*"

"You really love her, don't you?"

"Obviously! How can I not love her? She is beautiful. She is amazing. When she smiles, she squints her eyes. Her lips open and her teeth pop out.

You know, Mridula, whenever she wants to dictate terms to me, she locks a pen between her upper lip and her nose, and speaks in a coarse voice that is way far from manly. I cannot stand her not talking to me; so she goes mute in the midst of a conversation just like that. She lets me crumple under the weight of that silence, before she giggles to end it, and then bursts into laughter," Rishi said.

"So you want to fix her, don't you?"

"I want to make her whole again, but I cannot find her missing pieces on my own."

"…so you want her to help you," Mridula almost sniffed. "You want her to heal herself, so that *you* can be with her."

Rishi did not overlook the contempt in her voice this time.

"Yes, I do. What is wrong with that? I love her."

"Nothing wrong. Just don't condemn her if she does not do it…"

"I know…"

"…because you are not entitled to it. To her efforts or to her."

"I know!" He almost screamed.

Maybe Mridula was doing the right thing. Maybe Rishi deserved that truth be told. But imagine asking for a spoon at your friend's place while you have dinner. And they throw it at you from the kitchen. It hits your nose, so hard blood spurts from it. *What is this*, when you exclaim, they say, *the spoon, just what you needed.*

Mridula did that always—choosing the harshest words to speak the most gut-wrenching truths. Especially when it came to men. Call it sadistic pleasure if you may, it had become her second nature.

She did not want to hurt Rishi, though, and she realized it soon enough. A spark of disgust ran through him like electricity.

You want to feel certain things alone, right?

You love someone, but the setting is against you. You rage against it for a while, but it is like hitting a wall. You fall down. You get hurt but you hit again. You keep hitting until you break yourself.

All the people who care for you ask you to let go, at times even compel you with promises. Others talk about you, with sympathy, contempt, or whatever. You push yourself into a shell so that none of it affects you. You shut your ears, close your eyes. You do not talk about it to your friends, do not let anyone see how withered you are within. You try as hard as you can to convince yourself more than anyone else that you are happy loving them without expecting it back.

You find yourself standing on that middle ground, with your love, the hurt and the realizations. You want to be there all by yourself.

"Don't feel bad about it. It is what it is," Mridula said—her best attempt at an apology. She fished out her diary from her handbag then. *A Wistful Woman's Chronicle,* it read.

"How about I read something to you? I wrote this one a few years ago—"

Tell me where can love be found.
In hearts that loved, it has been sought.
Empty hearts with scars profound
tell tales of when for love they fought.

Hearts that seek this venture's peak
know: threads of love are delicate.
Two hearts, though each adventure seek,
will only fall if resonate.

As majestic, as sublime,
but love is rare in essence prime,
breeds in hearts for hearts they find.
Requite comes seldom intertwined.

Tell me not it does not fade—
it's fancied not, it never dies.
Ask me not to chase its shade.
I am too broken for such lies.

Fills with hope while wraps despair,
you will be hooked when it deserts.
Has no rules, it is unfair.
The thing about love is it hurts.

She closed her diary, and silence fell upon them. As they stared at the shimmering, trembling water, Mridula scratched her nails against the railing, rubbing off her amethyst nail paint. Rishi bit the dead skin off his lips. Then they walked to the nearest bench and sat.

"I am sorry," she said, opening her arms and leaning in, "I was rude." They hugged.

Rishi's head then descended to her lap. As he lay on the bench, he shoved his face in her stomach. Mridula hunched over him, resting her chin at the back of his head, locking him gently in the hollow of her body.

"I am sorry, but no. I cannot stop believing. That's easy," Rishi said.

"What?" Mridula asked, caught unawares.

"Everybody 'wants', you know, true love. Everybody likes companionship that survives. Everybody wishes that they had someone who would not give up on them so easily, but how many of us are willing to give that?"

"Are you saying that in context of that girl…her name…"

"Sachi," he said. "No, your poem. It makes me feel cynical."

"Okay!"

Mridula must always have the last words. She hated confrontation, but continued listening to him.

"You know it's rare. Old School Love, intimate emotional companionship, and all those beautiful things. And while most people truly desire it, the truth is that it rarely happens to people, and only to people who fight for it and can give what they want.

And it's one thing to think you're capable of giving all that you seek, and a whole different thing to deliver when time comes.

You know what's easy? To believe that what you seek just does not exist. To sit in a glass case and comment on how its futile to look for it.

But to step outside of it, and risk getting hurt to find it? That's tough, and maybe that's the test."

The hole in her chest jumped a centimeter or two in diameter; Rishi's words were a slap of truth. Had she loved truly? Ever? The first time, yes, definitely. She gave her everything, didn't she? She eloped with him, knowing how bad it could be if they got caught. And what unfolded was even worse—he sold her for money.

What happened, though, when love came knocking the second time? What did she do? She feigned it, didn't she? Why did she destroy his life? Why? To get her own means?

"You know, Mridula, my mother, of all other things, has taught me this one very important thing—never stop believing, even when you don't feel like it. Faith is powerful…"

No. She did nothing. Nothing.

"…but sometimes, it's tough. Very, very tough…to believe," he sighed.

10

Majorda Beach, Goa. 9ᵗʰ July 2012. 6:00 A.M.

If it were a love affair, the wind played the rogue lover. Mridula's hair—the self-destructive mistress giver, hopelessly in love. It swayed to the point of hurting her scalp. And if she dared to drop off her shades, the sand would charge at her eyes.

Mridula wore a long, cover-up beach dress, with printed pink artwork all over, loose, but tied around her waist to outline her chiseled, gym built hour-glass figure. And of course, a hat to go with it—Ms. Vashisht never compromised with her style statement.

So what it was six in the morning? So what the dawn was just breaking, and the beach was empty?

As she walked towards him, he stood barefoot on the chilly, morning sand. Waves that crashed against his legs washed away the sand around his feet, burying them deep into the shore.

"Why so early in the morning?" The wind and the waves ate half her words.

"Don't we take ourselves too seriously, Mridula?" He screamed back.

"What do you mean?" She could lower her volume now.

"Is this your out-of-the-bed look?" Rishi smirked.

"*Uhh*…no!" Mridula mewled.

"Can you not break the chain, talk in questions?" Rishi retorted.

"What are the rules?"

"How irrelevant can you be?"

"Why so early in the morning?"

"Why can't you learn from the sun, and not sizzle *so early in the morning?*"

The sun hung behind Rishi's head like the holy light. As it grazed the outline of his silhouette, it made her wince. Mridula was game-on.

"Why do we take ourselves so seriously?" She asked.

"What makes you throw around sass like confetti?" They laughed.

"Where did you learn such crappy lines from?" She asked, breaking into a chuckle.

"*Ouch!*"

"And here I win!"

"Did I not tell you reactions were allowed? Did I not prohibit *statements* only?"

"New rules midway?"

"Oh, my game? My rules?"

"*Blah!* Fine. You win."

As Rishi sprang his arms in the sky to sprawl, his mouth opened wide in yawn. Mridula took off her shades, squinting so her eyelids could guard against the sand. As the wind grazed Rishi's face, his teeth cluttered. The chilly air slid inside his navy blue floral print shirt like a lover's hand in a winter night.

Yet, when a cross-armed, shivering Mridula rubbed her palms against her forearms, he unbuttoned that shirt and wrapped it around her. In his head, he was her contemporary gentleman, now wearing just a sleeveless T-shirt. His eyes watered, and he shrunk to a hunched, shivering little boy.

Whenever Mridula looked at Rishi, it filled her with euphoria. To her, he looked like hope. How could winning that stupid *talk in questions* game, or offering her his shirt make him happy? And his unwavering smile? He even thought she was a good woman, didn't he?

Although, how do you define *good*? Does everyone not have their own version of it? Whatever Rishi's *good* comprised, Mridula fit in it, she knew. How did that not then make her *good enough*—worthy of everything, worthy of his love?

"But really, why did you call me so early in the morning," she asked.

"I do not know. I just felt like spending some time with you. I like it," he smiled at her. Her heart leapt.

"So what's the plan?"

"The plan is not to be serious this morning. Actually, let's play something. You suggest, and be silly." Rishi said.

"*Umm*…let's play *Stapoo*," she said, after pondering for a while.

"Okay, how do you play that?" He asked.

"It is a Rajasthani game. I used to play it when I was young."

"*Oh!* Rajasthan, nice. My grandparents live there."

"I know right. You were born there," she said.

"No. I was born in Indore, where my parents live."

"What? No. Who told you that," she blurted out.

"My mother, why?"

"Nothing!" *So! She had lied to him!*

"I used to play it all the time…then I turned twelve," Mridula covered.

"Why, what happened at twelve?" He asked.

Girls, after twelve, could not go to school or play in the open. She did not say that. She picked a pebble instead, and chose a plot on the beach, so far from the sea the waves did not even hanker to reach. She pressed the pebble deep in sand and started tracing the *Stapoo* arena—a large square border, divided into five rectangular grids. The third and the fifth grids subdivided into two halves, one for each foot—the player could rest there.

"The rules are simple," she said.

"Let me explain.

- You aim at each grid. One by one, you throw the pebble in each grid, from here, outside.

- You hop one-footed grid after grid to bring back the pebble.

- If the pebble touches any line, a foul happens. Same if you do while hopping.

- Every time a foul happens, turns switch. Until then, you keep covering grids.

- Whoever covers all the grids first wins."

"Cool! That is simple. Let's make it more fun. Just a slight addition."

"What?" She asked.

"Each time you commit a foul, you'll have to tell something about yourself. It can be a truth. It can be a lie. The other person has to guess. You may or may not reveal if it's a truth or a lie." He said.

"Sounds fun. Bring it on," she said.

"Ladies first?"

"The plan is to not be conventionally boring this morning." She squinted her eyes at him.

"Yeah, okay, fine." Rishi threw the stone first. It landed on the line.

"*Uff!*" She exclaimed, clapping her hands. Why did she behave like a child with him?

"Okay! My turn. I don't know how to flirt…" he said. And before he could finish, Mridula burst into laughter.

"Hey…yeah…okay…stop. Stop laughing, Mridula, how mean! Hey…stop…please." She did not stop.

"I choose not to reveal," he said, embarrassed but giggling all the same.

"So this incident happened in college," he said, as Mridula continued her struggle to not laugh.

"TEDx is a really cool department in my college. In the inductions, they had this questionnaire, where the last question was to write a pick up line. Brownie points for someone who comes up and says that to a senior girl."

"Okay, okay. Go ahead…"

"Now I want to make clear that all writers have this writer's ego. You must be original all the time."

"Okay…"

"…But the problem was that I did not know how to write a pickup line. So I wrote a pickup PARAGRAPH!" She laughed hard again.

"*Eh!* Will you listen?"

"Yeah okay, sorry, sorry. Say…"

"So I went up to her and said that, and walked out with brownie points and a puffed chest—I had conquered the territory. Later that day, I met my senior friend Zafar, who asked, 'Were you the one to say that pickup line to Rhea?' I said yes. He said, 'She was talking about you.' I asked what she said, and he said…"

Rishi took a dramatic pause. An imaginary DRUMROLL!

"'She ripped your ass,' he said." At that, she laughed so hard her bowels hurt. This time Rishi joined her.

"My means were a little embarrassing, but I got the brownie points. The job was done."

"Yeah! Yeah! Whatever."

It was Mridula's turn now. She crossed three grids, easy-peasy. Her toe kissed a line while returning from the fourth.

"Okay, *Ummmm*…I," she said.

"That is a lie, straightaway."

"But I haven't said anything."

"Whatever you're going to say is a lie."

"*Haww!* Am I such a liar, Rishi?" A puppy face she made.

"Well…" He shrugged. They chuckled.

"I…I am thirty-seven," she said.

"See…lie."

An unwavering stare from Mridula, and her smirk.

"Thirty-seven?" He asked.

"Thirty-seven."

"What? No, I mean, you don't look thirty-seven. I mean…you look much younger."

"What if I told you I have a child your age?"

"*Eh! Bhak!* I won't believe anything and everything," he rolled his eyes, as he stooped to pick his pebble.

"Yeah! That would be too far-fetched," she chuckled.

"My turn," Rishi said.

"Go ahead!"

Rishi crossed four grids this time. When he targeted the fifth grid though, the stone touched the line.

"*Ah*…what should I talk about? Nothing's really popping up…"

"Talk about anything…your family…your mother."

"My mother is my hero." Rishi said.

"What?"

"I love to talk about my mother…My mother is a different character all together. She is gullible, paranoid, loving, caring, everything at once. Mridula you know, she…"

He went on and on and on…

When he stopped, Mridula threw the pebble. It landed on the line, just short of the fifth grid. The hole in Mridula's chest was growing again.

"I want to leave…" she said.

"…and that's a lie." Rishi frowned.

"It's true," she said, and started walking away.

11

Indore, Madhya Pradesh.
11ᵗʰ August 2012. 9:41 A.M.

"What? He surrendered? But why!" Rishi exclaimed.

"I don't know, *beta*…I am very, very scared. We cannot get a bail for him. God only knows what *paap* I am reaping, *beta*." Sugna started weeping.

"*Maa* I'm taking a bus to Indore tonight. Don't cry, things will be fine," Rishi said, and cut the call. Sugna swallowed a lump. Was it right to call him so early? Now Rishi was tensed too.

Sugna was a desert woman, the only child to her parents. Her father ploughed a small piece of land in Nanarwara, Rajasthan. Her mother, just like all mothers, had taught her how to make a home. A *beendni* must know how to run the house, must cook food, must always wear a *ghunghat* outside her bedroom. Inside, however, it must never be a thing. As she dressed after a shower, the loose end of her saree that draped across her chest must subtly slide off her shoulder. Note: subtly. Her wet hair must be tied into a bun—men had a thing for bare, watery backs. And as she turned, her sweaty, watery chest must gloss at him.

It runs a shiver between his legs, her mother said. Her blouse must have hooks in the front, not at the back. So when the seduction peaked, he could clasp it in his fist and jerk it off. No bra, mind her.

However, she must do this every third or fourth night. The rest of the nights, she must let him crave her, chase her. So when it happened, it felt like she had given in. He must never know she had wanted it all along, that she had led him.

Your beend must crave you so much he can never displease you. That's how you build a family, Sugna, she would say.

At 13, Sugna never took her mother seriously. Her father's *ladli*, she wore his saggy old shirts and cycled to his field with his lunchbox wrapped in her mother's *dupatta*. In the evenings, she played *gilli danda* in the streets, with boys. Mind you, she could beat any ass in that game. At 14, her girl friends had started getting married, but Sugna could hardly do any chore.

By 15, she had mastered the art of sweeping and mopping the floor. But cooking daal? Or rice that was not wet? Or *chapattis* that were round? Or any dish that could water her *beend's* mouth? Sugna could not do any of that. All her friends had gotten married. While she was still her father's *ladli*, the resentment in her mother's eyes had begun to sting her.

At 16, the village started talking about her. *Pakhiya der kar raha hai. Chhori ki umar nikalti jaa rahi hai.* In hushed voices and mellow chuckles, her pregnant girl friends would discuss the things their husbands did with them in the bedroom. The giggles settled inside her like the gurgles of a ship sinking in an ocean as deep as her heart.

It was not like his father had not tried to get her married? Many a boy had come to see her, but Sugna was taller than half of them. And she wore loose shirts, did not cook, and played with the boys. *Chhora nahi hua, toh chhori ko hi chhora bana diya!*

It was not until she saw her father's love for her change that she shook. One afternoon, when she was 17, her father jerked the lunchbox from her hands. Looking away, in a cold voice, he said, *kalse tu ghar par hi rahegi.* Sugna had wept the entire night.

The next morning, she woke up at five. Her broom reached every little corner of her overfilled one-room *kuccha* hut; her mop pressed on the floor more than normal. When her mother woke up, Sugna groaned in sweat and back ache, but her house was clean. In the kitchen, her *rotis* were nearer to round than they had ever been. Her *chawal* was less wet, her *daal* less watery. Her mother knew something in her daughter had changed.

Sugna had sworn to become the finest figure of a *beendni*.

At 19, a news travelled in the village—*Pakhiya ke ghar Deewan Sahab aaye hain*. Sugna's efforts had so wondrously reaped fruits. The richest man in Pindwada had come to seek her hand in marriage for his son. For the first time in years, her parents were happy, and proud of her.

In the first night of marriage, though, her husband did not touch her. Sugna tried seduction, with her wet hair and a bare, watery back, but he did not touch her.

Her heart broke. How could she help not feeling like a prostitute?

Even when he did touch her, only flesh rubbed against flesh. It felt nothing like love. To the world, her marriage had everything. But to be loved by your man? Was that not important?

Her mother said it was not. *Aurat ko thoda toh sehna padta hi hai.*

But was he not supposed to crave her so much he could never displease her?

Tu koshish karti reh, she would say.

So she kept trying. Months passed, then years, but nothing changed. Even her mother-in-law did not like her. Who could she complain to? Her life became two grains of happiness in a bushel of compromises. But Sugna was a desert woman—she knew how to make compromises to hold her family together.

In all of this, she did not know when Rishi became her respite. All she wanted to be was a good mother. She did not know when he became to her the face of love. Hell broke loose upon her whenever he got sick. In his exam days, she would fast for him. And on the days they fought, sleep would be a far cry for her.

What did this woman have, but for her family?

The other night, her husband had surrendered to the police, admitting to have killed his father. Greed for property, he had said. But had he not always hated his legacy?

Sugna's world was closing in on her. She was very, very scared.

12

Panjim, Goa. 11th August 2012. 8:47 P.M.

…not a shirt on my back,
not a penny to my name.
Lord I can't go back home,
this away…

…I'm five hundred miles away from home…

…played on the stereo, as the driver pressed the power button on Mridula's request. Silence fell.

Mridula must reach the Panjim bus stand by nine, lest she should miss Rishi. He had to leave for Indore that night. Ranvijay had surrendered to the police, claiming to have killed his father—a non-bailable offence, to say.

Had she not seen it coming, though? *A weak man, through and through. I knew it,* she muttered through gritted teeth.

In the morning, he was so scared his voice faltered like anything. And why should he not be—his childhood had lurched into precocity in a flurry. He needed to talk to someone, and of all the people, he had chosen to call her. Not anyone else. Her.

The driver cut sharp right into another Goan lane— narrow, dusky, lined with trees and one-storey red, yellow and purple Portuguese houses. One last time, wasn't it? One last time of seeing Rishi, whose life she had irreparably squandered? Why did she do it? How would she explain it, *haan*? Collateral damage? The black hole in her chest popped bigger again.

She would hug him. Or would it be too much? If he got that close, if their bodies touched like that, would her guilt seep through? Would he sense that she was the reason? What would he think of her then?

No. She could not fall from grace in his eyes. When she was gone, he must not speak of her any less than how he spoke about Sugna—with glimmer in his eyes, sugar in his voice. O how he spoke of her!

"You know, Mridula, she randomly walks into my room and starts massaging my legs. But she would never let me massage hers. And sometimes she makes me damn angry. You know, once a lizard fell on the kitchen slab, beside my glass of milk. She didn't let me drink it; it may have poisoned it. But she drank it herself, lest the milk should be wasted.

And when I scolded her, she tried to evade it with her not so funny jokes."

"*Achha hi hoga na*, if I die," he would mewl. "She is too much sometimes, but she is cute," he would say, smiling mindlessly.

Would he talk like that about her, after reading what she had written for him?

Mridula must stop thinking of Sugna, lest the hole in her chest should tear through her body. Sugna was one thing Mridula could never be, a woman capable of selfless love. Although, could Sugna do any different? What do the weak do anyway—accept all the treachery, never avenge, just *love*?

Stupid woman! Stayed silent through everything, called it love. Mridula sniffed to herself.

How unlike Sugna she was! At seventeen, in an empty street in the middle of the night, she had picked herself. No man, no one had ever trampled upon her again. No one had ever dictated terms to her, not even fate. And look how she had detached herself from her past. Nothing could haunt her, pester her, because she chose peace. Mridula Vashisht made her own choices.

Although, if everything was a choice, could she have chosen any different? Maybe after being abandoned in that street, she did not have to go to the nearest town and seduce a marble shop owner into appointing her as his personal assistant. Just so she could eye on his clients— the wealthiest builders from Jaipur. Just so she could sleep with one of them, enchant him with her 'love' and have him employ her as the head waitress in one of his hotel ventures. Just so she could meet more men of consequence, lure them into bed, have them take her across the world.

Just so she could play around with them as she relished their wealth. Just so she could loot them of money, power and love, then ghost them and find another prey. O the predator she was!

Maybe she did not have to wage a war against the universe, and ravage its men to avenge herself. If everything was a choice, maybe she could seduce a man into loving her…and love him back? Maybe? Maybe she could channel that love towards her broken parts? Maybe she could start a family, have a child to love, a home to make?

But men cannot love. If you do not crush them, they crush you. How could her seduction ever cause such a fundamental change?

Maybe there was a way to detach from her past, which did not involve killing two men, costing a dozen lives, including Rishi's, as collateral damage. Or maybe not.

No. Love was for the weak. Love was, but, for the weak.

Was it, though? The other night, when Rishi had hugged her, he had missed the tears in Mridula's eyes she would do everything to not let fall. When he had laid his head in her lap, she was melting. When had she ever melted like that after ghosting or inflicting pain upon a man? How could something, if not mightier than her, ever melt her like that?

As the cab halted, Mridula's head hit the headrest of the front seat. Rishi stood at a distance, buying a ticket from the bus conductor. *Aparajita Travels*, read his orange bus, in big italic font. She got out of the car and asked the driver to wait for her.

No. No. No. She had not chosen to do anything. After she was abandoned, she was filled with angst, disgust, and pain. Everything had to come out, and that is how it did.

But did Sugna not have similar pain, similar angst? Maybe much less profound, but similar. Why did she, then, love, unlike Mridula?

Love and kindness were choices only the bravest of hearts could make. And Sugna was much stronger than Ms. Mridula Vashisht.

"Mridula?"

What was Mridula, a damsel? O what a damsel she was!

Whatever, her horrible existence had caused tremendous chaos in the world, and nothing but pain to the people she never wanted to hurt. The hole in her chest dilated to the brink of bursting. She could hardly speak.

So when she reached Rishi, she said nothing. She pushed herself up on her toes and wrapped her arms round his neck. He must have heard her hisses, or sobs.

"Mridula?" Rishi said, surprised, hugging her back. When she separated, she reached out to his laptop bag and slipped into it her diary of poems, *A Wistful Woman's Chronicle*.

"Wow…wait. Why this diary? It is so precious to you…" She covered his lips.

"Something for you to remember me by," she said. "You will remember me na, Rishi?"

"Of course, Mridula. I will come back soon. We will talk."

"Don't forget me, Rishi. Please don't…"

"I won't Mridula…" The bus honked. She hugged him for one last time.

As he got on board, the conductor closed the door.

A…P…A…R…A…J…

Each letter whizzed past her as the bus moved. When it was gone, she took to the nearest bench and let her feet give way.

Rishi was gone.

ONE HOUR LATER

"May I switch on the music ma'am?" asked her cab driver, and this time Mridula did not miss his white complexion. Vintage English music too, but no English accent. Not that she cared.

Mridula nodded. She did not mind the music. She did not mind anything anymore.

…If you miss the train, I'm on.
You will know that I have gone.
You can hear the whistle blow,
a hundred miles…

"My mother is English, ma'am," he said. Who asked him that? A hippie decided to settle for an Indian penis, bore this dickhead. Mridula did not say anything.

It would take twenty minutes to reach her resort—it was time. She fished into her handbag for her bottle of tranquillizers, which she had lured a waiter into arranging for her the other day. By the time she reached the terrace, they would be at their peak effect. As the driver looked at her gulp down half the bottle, it did puzzle him. But he said nothing, of course.

By the time she reached, her vision had blurred, her mind hazed. *Purple Vine Villa*, she could not read. As she made her way through the gate, with faltering wobbly steps, the guard must have taken her for drunk—very generic of high class women.

On the terrace now. The sparkling cityscape of Panjim failed to charm her as she lit a cigarette for herself. Her eyes could not shake from the orange, burning end of it. Every time she dragged, the orange sizzled into a bright, golden shade. Each time, it made her laugh. Why did she laugh? What was funny?

After a few drags, her stomach churned. Was it the cigarette, or the pills? Who cared?

The pills were mild; half a bottle would not kill her. However, once she hit the ground, they would make sure she could not be saved. Beneath her lay the swimming pool—no guards. No one should watch her falling.

When the white part of the cigarette had burnt, she pressed it against the railing. Her bowels begged her to throw up, but she would not. Instead, she would stand on the railing now. Mridula must look death in the eye before it took her.

Could she, though? Standing still had never been more difficult.

Huh! Mridula Vashisht could do anything. She raised her left foot on to the railing and pushed herself upon it. She now sat doubled up on the railing, pendulating like a hit-me toy. As she tried to stand, though, her foot slipped.

Mridula was falling.

No. Oh god! No! She could not slip like that. She wanted to stand, her arms wide open, like the Jesus's cross or Kate Winslet from The Titanic. She wanted to choose when she would surrender.

Oh god! Please! No! She had slipped, just like that. She did not want to die *just like that*. God! Please! Could she have a retake? Please…please…please…

Mridula hit the ground, so hard it blew life out of her. As she lay against her chest, blood flew out of her head, upon the grained, black marble floor, mixing with dust.

Mridula Vashisht was dead.

13

Indore, Madhya Pradesh.
15th August 2012. 2:37 P.M.

Rishi's finger grazed the rough patch of the otherwise well-fabricated cover, where she had written *A Wistful Woman's Chronicle*. Independence Day, it was; not until the next day could he do anything about his father's bail. As he lay in his bed with heavy, frantic thoughts, he leafed through its pages. She called it a chronicle for a reason—it had poems with dates, and little contexts from her life below them.

But A Wistful Woman? It was not fair of her to call herself that, Rishi thought. *And why would she let me read all this?*

Rishi skimmed through the diary, reluctant to read any context because it was personal to her.

Until he reached the page bookmarked with the ribbon. It did not have a poem, but a letter. A letter addressed to him.

11ᵗʰ August, 2012.

Dear Rishi,

You must be wondering why I left you this precious diary of mine. Well,

a) I could not think of a better parting gift. I am leaving for Amsterdam, never to return. I love that city.

b) I had a few things to say.

Thank you for being my best friend. For that alone, you deserve to know my truth.

I come from your village, Rishi, Mandwada Khalsa. My father led a musical group that played for its patron royalty, your grandfather. He held my father in very high regard.

So when I eloped, my parents ran to your grandfather for help, and he did not disappoint them. He managed to track us in no time. He could have beaten the boy to death, but the boy claimed outright that he loved me.

So your grandfather decided to play with it. He offered him a deal—he could flee with me or let them take me for loads of money. Did young, petty love even stand a chance there?

He did not return me to my parents either. After all, I had acted like a free bird; my wings must be clipped. And he was a lusty beast. So he raped me.

He did realize, though, that he had a lot to lose. So he proposed to my parents that I married his munim. Ashamed by my deed, my parents were more than happy to accept. Deewan Sahab toh Bhagwaan hain!

My fifty-six-year-old husband would beat me every night, just for fun. I slept under his bed, seldom spoke a sentence and endured his nasty words and gazes. To love and to dream was to sin; I had understood that.

That is why I could never love Ranvijay. Yes, your father. He loved me; he still does. When I returned, he was the first person I met. They had told him I had demanded money of them and fled. When I told him the truth, he lost control. I had never seen him in such a fit of rage. He poisoned your grandfather.

Don't hate him, Rishi. He was never like this. He used to be so full of life he would fill the entire mansion with vivacity. I worked as a maid for your grandmother. That is where I had seen him first. When he had come to talk to me, I had avoided him at first. I was scared they would beat me up. You know, a weak woman is always guilty.

A few conversations later, though, we became friends. Your grandma hated that, but he would fight with her for me, always. He had fallen in love with me, I could tell. I had not, but he could help me escape.

So when he confessed, I did not refuse.

He was very fond of me. He remanded people who shouted at me, even my husband, many a time. He bought me chocolates with his pocket money savings and saved the most beautiful ghaghra for me from the lot that came for servants on festivals. I liked all his gestures. I liked him very much, but I did not love him.

But one afternoon, in a moment of passion, we committed a sin. We slept, and I conceived. I was seventeen then.

I was scared. I had thought Ranvijay would abandon me, but he did not. Instead, he claimed outright that he loved me. To my surprise, your grandmother took a sudden liking to me too. She started calling me beta and curating my diet plan. She even fed me with her own hands sometimes. Can you believe?

They made my husband divorce me. It all felt like a dream—having a caring family, a husband who loved, and a child that I was carrying within me. Had I ever wanted anything more than that?

Ranvijay and I had been told I was about to be a mother to the family's waris. Once I gave birth to the child, they would marry us. Ranvijay was happier than I was. And to my realization, I had started to like him even more. Love, was it? I do not know.

Nine months later, my water broke. I had given birth to a boy…you.

The delivery had been normal, but I was exhausted. Your grandma took you outside, and the midwives gave me a potion that put me to sleep.

When I woke up, though, I was on some street, without you, without Ranvijay, all alone. The dream was over.

Why had I not realized it sooner that they did not want me, that they just wanted you? I lay in the middle of I did not know where, with a body yet to recover and a soul dead. That was when I decided—love was for fools.

One summer night, when he was fourteen, Rishi had woken up in the middle of the night with a desiccated throat. As he had walked down the stairs to fetch himself some water, his legs had frozen outside the kitchen.

"Barah saal ho gaye. Rijhati kyu nahi, baanjh hai kya?" His grandma had retorted his mother.

Did it even make sense? What *barah saal*, Rishi himself was fourteen? And *baanjh*? Oh my god! That night he had decided—he hated his grandmother.

I will not claim to be your mother, Rishi. I don't deserve it.

In all fairness, Sugna is your mother. She is equally wronged as I, if not more, but her choices make her much stronger a woman than I can ever be. She has taught me this one thing—no matter how hurt we are, we can always choose love and kindness over the incessant urge to destroy the world in vengeance.

My choices have been very different. When I rose from that trauma, I became Mridula Vashisht—the heartless, irresistible woman who promised love to men and ghosted them.

That is the thing, Rishi. We think we are too significant to the universe. We believe the things we do and the things that happen to us shake the balance of the universe when they do not. I thought I deserved revenge. I set out to loot men, hoping I would find peace. But I never really found it. Wherever I went, my past kept following me, haunting me. It pushed me into an existential crisis—was I intrinsically an immoral woman, or just a tremendously oppressed person gone berserk?

So I went on a killing spree.

But Sugna? What did she choose? She could have become a vindictive stepmother, but she chose to love you. When her life lacked meaning, she sought it in raising you. She has given, and continues to give, her everything to you, to Ranvijay, to her family.

But Rishi, your mother abandons herself. And why would she not? Everyone that should have loved her—her parents, her new family, Ranvijay—all of them have abandoned her. She has never known any different, so she finds it tough to believe she can be loved.

And you, my boy, have been raised with it. You have seen it so closely you mimic that. That is why when Sachi could not love you, you could not detach it from yourself. You have been fighting for her love, just so it validates what you otherwise find it tough to believe—that you deserve to be loved and fought for. Look how you abandon yourself.

Rishi, think of the steady, nurturing, healing love you give out. Promise me you will give that to yourself. Promise me you will teach yourself, and your mother, to accept nothing less than that. When I saw you at your grandfather's funeral, I started melting. When they had thrown me out of the village, I had thought I had lost my innocence forever. But then I met you, and I felt it alive, breathing in you.

So promise me you will protect it. Promise me you will not make the same mistakes as I did. Promise me you will not seek vengeance from the world, but channel that energy inwards to fix yourself and your family.

Maybe then I will have redeemed myself.

Love and apologies,
Mridula Vashisht.

14

Indore, Madhya Pradesh.
16ᵗʰ August 2012, 8:02 P.M.

"You know you're very lucky, right?" Sachi retorted as she came with the cigarettes Rishi had asked her to fetch. Her parents were not home; her brother did not mind his visit at eight in the evening.

"*Hmm*," Rishi nodded.

They stood at the terrace of Sachi's lavish three-storey bungalow, their legs tucked between the bars of its metallic railing. In the middle of it was a fountain with lights that changed colours. Its base looked like an artist's colour palette; beams of blue, red and yellow scattered in the water. Rishi stared vacantly at the city that had been home to him for years. The evening breeze made his eyes squint.

The city felt alien now. The parks where he played cricket, his school, the winding roads, narrow colony streets, the lesser-known pockets in the town—everything felt foreign as if he did not belong there.

"Rishi, don't do this," Sachi said, pressing the pack of *Marlboro* between her index finger and thumb.

"Why are *you* judging, *haan*?"

"I am not judging," she rolled her eyes. "I do it myself, but not like this."

"Like what?"

"I don't want it to become your coping mechanism."

"Don't lecture me today. Teach me how to smoke."

"Fine!" Sachi sniffed. "Do it by yourself. You don't need me to learn how to. *Huh!*" She handed the pack to him and stormed downstairs.

Rishi was too exhausted to bother. He pressed a cigarette between his lips and lit a matchstick, but the breeze would not let the flame survive. After five failed attempts, he managed to light his cigarette.

When he took his first drag, though, he knew he needed Sachi. His sinuses filled with smoke; his nostrils had to puff it out. He hated the ashy taste of it. As he coughed, he wondered how people got addicted to that burning piece of shit, and why Sachi liked it so much.

After a few drags, the uneasiness started settling. The drags became smooth; the puffs were now fun to him. Then the cigarette hit him, and his explosive thoughts turned mellow. He liked the buzz, and it was making sense to him now.

His mind had become a battlefield. His father—he had always been a terrible husband to his mother. In the same heart that had housed respect but also anger for him, pity was sprouting now. His mind raced to justify his father, but what would that make of his mother? Collateral damage?

About his mother, she was not really his mother. How would he unlearn that? What did he feel for her now? Overwhelming respect and transcendental love, but what about that itching feeling of otherness dangling from the bottom of his heart?

And Mridula? His friend of 'incompatible' age? Or his mother should he say? How could he miss her? How could he hate her either?

What would happen next? Would his father be out of the legal peril he had pushed himself into? How would he hold his mother up? Will they remain the same after what he had learnt? How would he restore his family?

He did not know any of that. All he knew was that he would. All he knew was that he had to. All he wanted right now was a moment's relief from the gut-wrenching pain of knowing things he did not want to know. All he wanted was to sit by the girl he loved, who did not love him back, but it did not matter. All he wanted was to let his heart sink until he could garner enough strength to pick himself up.

As his first cigarette burnt out, he chain-lit a second.

"No more of it, Rishi," dictated Sachi, her glare so intense her eyes almost popped out. She pulled the cigarette from between his lips and threw it away. She also snatched the pack from him.

"What?"

"No more cigarettes. Have this instead," she said, handing him a *cornetto*. She had one for herself too.

"Listen, I am not in the mood for an ice cream today. I want another one of those."

"The cigarette was to numb your head. The ice cream is to fix your soul. Have it, please?" She said with her gentle authority. How could Rishi ever stand that plea, that smile, the mellow voice of hers?

For good fifteen minutes, they said nothing. The ice cream seemed to do just what Sachi had deployed it for. Rishi's eyes had big, bulgy bulbs of tears now. With blurry eyes, he looked at Sachi, who was yet to finish her cone. She was cute, pure, untouched and innocent.

It's funny how the mind draws a line, how it splits time—Rishi would always remember life as *before* and *after* he learnt the truth. Just two days ago, he had had a family, an unhappy but normal family. His problems were first-world. Now, everything had changed.

"Just two days ago, Sachi, my mother was mine, and she was my only mother and…but now…" Rishi broke off and wept.

Sachi must have wanted to say the best things in the world at that moment, but she knew she would choke. Rishi was too fragile for that failed attempt right now. So she interlocked his arm tight in hers and pressed her cheek against it.

"Everything will be okay, Rishi. You're stronger than this," she said.

Maybe it was not love, but it soothed. It would never be anything beyond friendship, but why was that important? Why do we always want *the next step* to happen, when we know some of our bonds might break in the process? In that moment, they were friends, and it was enough.

"Let's have some music," Sachi said, releasing his arm.

"I don't have my earphones," Rishi replied.

"I have air pods," she said, extending one to him. She put the other in her right ear.

"Alan Walker?"

"Anything works for me," Rishi said.

"Alan Walker it is, then!"

She tapped on her phone; the music played. Rishi stared vacantly at the sky as she hummed to the lyrics of the song:

> *...If this night is not forever, at least we are together.*
> *I know I'm not alone. I know I'm not alone...*

Fireflies

1

When I was sixteen, *Ammi* would tell us stories with life lessons as she massaged our heads in the afternoons. Time fogged most of those teachings nonchalantly, but there is one that is still etched in my head.

In hearts of the people we love, we see reflections of ourselves, *Ammi* had said, as her oil-laced fingers clawed on Sabeena's scalp one afternoon.

I wanted to argue that it was not true, for whenever I looked at Sabeena, I only felt filthy. I felt guilty of shooing my little sister away whenever she talked to me with extra sugar in her voice, or behaved in front of *Ammi* as though she looked up to me. She often trailed after me round the village. It infuriated me when the villagers looked at us and smiled at the sisterly love that she made a spectacle of. I often turned around and shoved upon her words that would ooze out of my anger. Her face fell; tears swelled up at the corner of her eyes. Her lips fluttered like waves. It made me feel like the cheapest person on the planet, although I was a good sister.

Twelve years later, as I float in the air, a thousand feet above the ground, *Ammi's* words remain untrue. Twelve years have passed since I abandoned them—my *Ammi*, Sabeena, my village Rohila, my former life for that matter. She hates me for running away with Bhoomi, who she thinks was only my best friend. How could I ever tell her that she was my lover? How could I tell *Ammi* that her Adeeba was a lesbian? How could she accept a daughter who was an abomination to her Allah? Why would she?

I sit with Veer in the basket of his hot air balloon. The air is so cold it pricks my face and runs shivers down my body. As it rubs against my eyes, I squint. He puts his right arm around me. A shivering me fits perfectly in the hollow of his body. With his left hand, he thrusts the rope that hangs loose from the blast valve. Every time he does, fire springs out, heating the air in the balloon to keep us floating.

As he envelops me, I disconnect from the world outside his arms. I am slipping; I do not know why. My heart is pouncing. I am feeling the butterflies when I should feel nothing. I am praying to Allah, who I do not believe in—I am losing control. I am falling in love with Veer, but I swear it is not because he owns *WanderHeist*, the largest adventure sports franchise in the country. Or because his father is a billionaire. I am not a pretty, manipulative woman. I do not know why, but I beg you, this is not the reason. I am falling because, maybe, when I look into his eyes, I see a reflection of myself…and I do not hate it.

The sky above is crimson with falling dusk. My city, Manali, glitters beneath. I have worked as a tourist guide here for seven years now. When *Baba* had brought us here, I did not like this place. Not until I started roaming in its colourful streets. Not until *Baba* started telling me stories about *Shiva*, about *Hidamba* and the *Pandavas*, about godly wars and the eternal glory of truth winning over evil. Not until these stories immersed me in the history of this city. Not until I lived these stories as I drowned. I know this city inside out, all those enchanting landscapes that people travel miles for, and the not so beautiful places they hardly ever visit. In the holy temples, with steeples swimming in amethyst, spirituality transcends in people. The city has dirty little pockets too, where only lust and animal instincts prevail. You will find people who come from far off lands, who this city welcomes and opens all its beauty to. Then there are the natives of this place, who struggle to sustain themselves, who this city rejects every day.

I embed my face in his chest again and close my eyes. None of us says a word, but the silence does not bite. The commotion below has ceased; fire springing from the blast valve is all I hear now. My hair flutters against the gusts of his breath as he slides his fingers into mine.

As I pluck my head from his chest, he plants a kiss on my forehead.

"Thank you, Adeeba, for letting me bring you here," he whispers. I hardly chuckle before I press my face against his chest again. "It's beautiful," I manage to speak.

His lips leave a moist imprint on my forehead; the air renders that patch of my skin cold. The mountains around are capped with snow. Cones of deodar trees wrap their bases in a blanket of Sacramento green. Roads spiral around these mountains, railed to keep the beautiful abysses from swallowing lives. The river that flows over the rock bed beneath bisects the city. The paragliders, helicopters and hot air balloons descend as night falls. Rafts have returned to the banks, and people, with their families, retreat to their lodgings.

I cannot fall in love with him. No, I cannot. Love, for me, is like a moth; I have been its fire. It gets drawn to me because I have a pretty face. Whenever I have touched it, though, I have burnt it alive. *Ammi*, Sabeena, Bhoomi and *Baba*, everything my twenty-nine-year-old life has been until now—everything becomes a lie if this is true. What I feel right now is treachery to all of them. To Bhoomi, who does not even remember she ever kissed me—I have promised her I will love her forever. To *Ammi* and Sabeena—they did not have to lose me if I could love anyone else other than Bhoomi. Although, what I feel for Veer does not involve flesh and bones, only the soul.

To *Baba*—he did not have to sign up for a daughter like me. When he adopted us, all he wanted was the love of children that fate had denied him. He deserved two *normal* daughters. Normal—not an impaired woman with Anterograde Amnesia, or a lesbian me.

Ammi's words are not true, for I do not see any of this when I look into Veer's eyes.

The more I fall for him, the deeper I drown in self-loathing. If I let him love me, I will render him empty. No matter how beautiful a story he writes for me, I might burn all those pages. I have done this in the past. I will do it again, even though I want to love with all my soul, with everything I have this time.

How do I love him with everything I have, though? How do I, tell me, when my soul lives in a body that can only love a woman? And how do I resist it when it is so tempting? *Ya Allah*, save me from being selfish…yet again.

As I said, though, I am slipping. Chemicals overpower my conflicts; it is all pleasant.

The basket lands with a gentle jerk, which pulls me out of my train of thoughts. As we walk to his BMW, he clutches my hand. Even though my heart is sinking, I am smiling. My head is bursting with confusion, but there is little euphoria that makes everything worth the while. I know we will only hit a dead end, but the chemicals are popping. The thought is powerless.

I can see the storms that my feelings promise, but with his hand in mine, I feel unshakable.

2

"**U**ncouth, uncultured morons! *Mandir ke bahar sutta phoonkengey. Bhagwaan ka darr khatam ho gaya hai bilkul.* Don't you worry. *Mahadev* has kept everyone's *hisaab,*" *Baba* lets out an angry soliloquy as he bangs the door. I rush through my *namaz*, lest all of it should fall upon me. It is five in the morning.

"What happened, *Baba*?" I ask him, as he hands me his stick and shuts the door behind him. His breath is short from climbing the stairs, his muffler drenched in sweat. As he limps his way to the sofa, he presses his palm against his right knee, rendering his left leg as weightless as possible. He pulls up the leg of his pyjama, uncovering a swollen knee.

"*Ya Allah*! How did it happen, *baba*?"

"*Aaj kal ke bachhe*, Adeeba," he said, fuming. "I wonder why people don't educate their children about religion these days."

"But what happened?"

"Outside the Mandir, I saw three brats smoking. One of them leaned against the statue of *Nandi. Hey Bholenaath!* The audacity of your generation astounds me as much as it shames. I ran after them with my *lathi,* screaming meanwhile to draw everyone's attention towards them. They started running too, shamelessly laughing as if it were one big joke. *'Chacha, ganja hai ganja. Shivji ko bhi pasand hai.'* (Uncle, it's weed. Even Lord *Shiva* likes it).

I tripped over something and fell. *Wo toh umar ho gayi hai meri, warna bachte nahi.*" (But for my age, nothing could have saved them.)

I believe him on this. Several medals of honour hang from the wall to testify that. *Baba* was one of the fittest Police constables in Mahabaleshwar in his days. He retired nine years ago. After losing *Mataji* (a year after that), Mahabaleshwar smothered him. He wanted to live in the mountains, closer to Lord *Shiva.* So we sold off the little property he had there and bought this little house. Very small, but for *Baba, Bhoomi* and me, it is enough.

"One *haramzaada* was even wearing leather! *Chamri* in a Mandir!"

"*Baba.* Language!"

"*Huh!* Go bring me *haldi ka lep.*" He sniffs with a disgusted frown on his face. *Haldi ka lep* is the remedy always. My *Baba* for you.

Every morning, *Baba* wakes up at four without fail. He must do *Surya-namaskar* to the rising sun at Siyali Mahadev Mandir, a kilometre and a half away from where we live. He takes a bath and leaves for his morning errand. Before he does, however, he never misses to wake me up for my morning *namaz*.

He reminds me of *Ammi* sometimes. On the days I sprawl in bed for long, he sprinkles cold water on my face. He sometimes even slaps me, as hard as he can without crumpling under his fatherly love. My *Baba* is the most chivalric man I have ever met.

Besides being chivalric, *Baba* is also a religious man. Now that he is out of duty, he immerses himself in holy scriptures. When I am out showing places to tourists, he sits with Bhoomi and reads to her *Shrimad Bhagwat Geeta*. He says it teaches the right way to live one's life. Of course, he has to reiterate every fifteen minutes, but he never loses patience with her.

On the days I am home, I lay my head in his lap as he narrates to me anecdotes of Lord *Shiva's* glory, of which some are my favourites. His stories are so diverse, colourful and triumphant they intrigue me. I love the story of *Neelkanth*, how during *Samudra Manthan*, the *Devas* (gods) and *Asuras* (demons) churned the ocean of milk to get the *Amrit* (The Elixir of Life). The first thing to appear was a dark sticky foam, the poison *Halahala* that had the power to destroy the Universe. When its fumes spread in the air and water, *Mahadev* drank it whole to save the world. *Devi Parvathi* caught hold of his neck to keep the poison from descending into his body, turning his throat blue. That is why he is also called *Neelkanth*.

"If he can drink poison to save the world, he can also perform *Tandava* (the dance of fury) and open his third eye to destroy it. One must always watch their actions," *Baba* would say. I do not love these stories for the sake of stories. I love them because his gods respect their wives; because his religion has women goddesses.

Unlike mine. As kids, we could not enter mosques without a *burkha*. But *Maulvi Sahab* sometimes exempted men from covering their heads even.

Also, when *Baba* narrates them to me, he lights up— the spark on his face, the zeal in his eyes. A sense of pride in his faith. I love these stories because they come from a man who can accept a Muslim daughter and never ask her to change her religion, despite being so ethnocentric himself.

I do not believe in Allah. After all these years, after everything that has happened, how can I? But *Baba* wakes me up every morning to offer *namaz*. I go to mosques, do *sajdah* to Allah, and every other thing *Baba* knows Islam obligates me to do. I do everything without belief just so *Baba* shall be proud of me. He always says, "*When we abandon our faith and assume supreme mastery over ourselves, we are headed towards our own doom.*"

I will not tell you I have never broken rules. I have, all the time, but never in front of *Baba*. Maybe that is why he does not know my reality.

After I massage his knee with that *lep*, he lays down on his bed. Bhoomi is not awake yet. I stare vacantly at the street in front of me. There is a vendor who sells *channa madra* every morning, some people in tracksuits and mufflers out on morning walks, everything divided into a thousand little pieces by the mesh on my window. It is fifteen minutes to seven now.

My thoughts teleport me to a point in time when the most horrid things in my past had not happened to me. I lived in Rohila, a small village in the heart of Maharashtra, with *Ammi* and my little sister Sabeena. In the afternoons, *Ammi* would do *champee* to our hair with coconut oil.

I hated it when Sabeena sat beside me as I painted. Since we had no money to afford hobbies, I would draw on ruled notebook sheets instead of drawing canvas, with pencil colours that I managed to pilfer from my classmates' schoolbags. She would clasp the pencils between her palms and watch me draw with sheer enthusiasm. Whenever I lifted my hand from the sheet, she put forward her spectacle of not so varied shades of pencils for me to choose from.

I swear I was a good sister. If I were not, I would not care for her the way I did. Sabeena was twelve. She still peed in her bed, and by bed, I mean mattresses laid on the floor. When *Ammi* woke up in the morning, she would paint her skin red with bruises. She believed, alike every other villager, it to be a sin against Allah to defecate or urinate where you lived and ate. Food and shelter were sacred. *Ammi* said Sabeena was old enough to control herself.

Ammi was very puritanical that way. When I was young, I had gotten beaten up dozens of times for not wearing a *hijab* to school. After *Abbu's* demise, though, she had eased out a bit. Her daughters' religious obligations had ceased to be her primary cause of concern, since she had a family to feed.

The first two times she found Sabeena's bed wet, she beat her until she was profusely crying. She never found anything after that. I would check on Sabeena every night. Whenever she was wet, I lifted her slightly and shifted her to my bed, taking good care not to wake her up. I would tiptoe out of the house with the mattress. Behind the southern wall, I had tied a rope. I had a spare pot, and a stock of firewood which I refilled from time to time. The mattress took half an hour to dry up.

In the nights she woke up, she walked behind me to the rope without saying anything. She knew she was making me suffer. When we were back in bed, she would push me a little and lay beside me, wrapping her arm tightly across my belly, almost embedding her face in my chest. "Thank you, Adeeba *Appi,* for saving me yet again. You are Allah's best gift to me. *Alhamdulillah!* I can even eat stones if you ask me to," she would say. In that moment, I forgot everything and held her tightly in my arms. She was my little sister. I loved her.

In the streets Sabeena had a knack for picking up fights. When I say fights, I do not mean verbal arguments with girls of her age that ended in pulling of ponytails. In fact, all the girls in the village liked Sabeena. She was a mini women rights' activist.

One evening, I was wandering in the streets when my eyes fell upon Sabeena with her girl gang. She had a cricket bat in her hand, with which she thrashed a boy left and right. I had resolved fights for her before, but there had never been anything of such intensity. The boy could retaliate, for he was much older, almost my age. His friends stood some distance away. Their teeth were cluttering, because it is only chivalric of men to not hit women. (Unless you marry her, of course.)

One of the girls told me the boy had written a letter for me. He had asked Sabeena to hand that letter to me. Bits of paper lay scattered on the ground, crumpled and torn haphazardly.

I clasped Sabeena's hand and started walking. My grip was so tight it must have hurt. I was fuming.

"*Appi,* listen to me please. That boy…he was…"

"Shut up! Sabeena. Not…a…word."

When we reached home, I wrested her hand such that she was thrown onto the bed. Thankfully, *Ammi* was still at the construction site. I did not want her to see that and beat Sabeena up. I did not talk to her though. For the rest of the day, she did not even try. At night, she came up to me when I was making beds. She offered to help me and I could not refuse, lest *Ammi* should notice. She tried to slip in a conversation too, but I gave her a glare and she stopped.

When Sabeena was asleep, I turned towards her. I loved looking at her when she slept. When she was born, I had not stopped jumping until I had gotten a cramp in my right leg. I had issued strict instructions regarding how to handle her, how to change her diapers, when and how to feed her so the morsel did not slip into her windpipe, and how to lift her, which I let happen only in extreme cases. When she was three-and-a-half years old, I used to wash her clothes and prepare her for school every morning. At school, it was me the teachers confronted for her fighting tendencies. I had taught her how to read the Quran, how to offer *namaz* to Allah, and how to write without breaking the nib of the pencil. I had also taught her alphabets, numbers, addition and subtraction. *Ammi* often said I was her second mother; it never failed to puff my chest with pride.

It feels like yesterday when I lived with *Ammi* and Sabeena, and life was simple.

3

The sky is an infinite platter of Prussian blue, with a million sparkling dots sprinkled upon it like stardust. *Ammi's* words jam my head: *In hearts of the people we love, we see reflections of ourselves.*

Veer clutches my hand as if I would slip away otherwise. As we approach the temple, one stair at a time, the temperature slithers from chilly to pleasant. When we are close enough, steam from the hot water spring starts condensing on our noses, faces and hands. The *Vashishtha temple* stands in front of us. There is an elevated platform towards the side, where the mountain goes downslope. Below is my city, embellished with lights of yellow, red and all other colours. Above, a sky full of stars. To choose which looks more beautiful is the most pleasant misery.

Every night we go out, he brings me here. We sit with our legs hanging, in the company of just each other—

Veer's idea of romance (mine too). He does not stop once he starts talking. I love listening to him.

The seven prominent stars you see at night, the *Saptarishi*, represent seven Rishis. One of them was Rishi Vashishtha, to whom this temple belongs. The Hindu god Ram was a student to him. Legends have it that his brother Lakshman had shot an arrow in the ground. It caused this hot water spring to appear, so Rishi Vashishtha did not have to go somewhere else to bathe. The temple is four thousand years old.

Of course, Veer does not know any of this. His fondness for this place stems solely from its aesthetics—golden walls, wooden artwork, the pleasant temperature because of the hot water spring. If I start with my trivia, he will crib,

"Stop it, babes! You're not on duty."

"What is babes, *eh*?" I laughed. "And how can the history of this place not intrigue you?"

"Why should it?" He says, frivolously playing with my hair.

"*Arre!* Doesn't it fascinate you? To think of how this place must be a hundred years ago? Or two hundred years ago. What if Laxman had not shot that arrow? This place would not even have been here. Just imagine!"

"Bleh! No, it doesn't. All that matters is that it's beautiful. Just look at it, Adeeba!" He opens his arms to the abyss.

"*Huh!*" I scoff.

"Is that why you became a tourist guide?"

"Partly yes! I mean, I love digging up the history of places and things…even books, you know. I must be the only person on the planet who's more obsessed with the author who wrote a book than the book itself."

"*Hmm*, so you're a gold digger!"

"What…why? *Huh*?"

"Yeah, old is gold. And you like digging up what's like…*umm*…four thousand years old?" He says, pointing at the temple. I slap him in the arm.

"Pathetic…pathetic attempt at being funny," I spit. We chuckle.

"No, but seriously, why did you become a tourist guide?"

"My *Baba* used to tell me stories about Hinduism. They used to fascinate me. When we moved to Manali, the beautiful history of this place consumed me."

"Hmm. Interesting."

"Why did you choose this adventure sports thing?" I ask him.

"I have reincarnated from a vulture," he says. I laugh. "*Arre!* It's true. I carried that thing for flying from my past life," he finishes, smirking. I slap him in the arm again.

We settle down, and he lights a cigarette for himself.

"Light one for me too," I say, still fidgeting from the cold.

"What? Cigarette? You?"

"Why? You won't allow that?"

"No. Pardon me. I am just taking a moment to digest that my girlfriend is savage."

"Am I, though?"

"What, savage?"

"No, your girlfriend." We laugh. He lights a cigarette for me.

"Good. Now teach me how to smoke." This time, he is alone in his laughter.

"What? *Arre*…Do as I say. *Huh!*"

"Okay…Okay…wait," he said, still laughing. "You are adorable, Adeeba!"

"Yeah. Whatever," I roll my eyes at him. He holds the cigarette between the tips of his index finger and thumb and brings it close to my lips. "Press this between your lips but don't lick it. Suck from it as you would suck from a straw," he says.

The first time I do it, my sinuses burst with smoke. I cough hard, but he is patient. After coughing my lungs out a few more times, it starts happening.

After our cigarettes burn out, we sit in silence. As he leans back, his arms stand like pillars to carry his body against the ground. My eyes water against the chill in the air; the incandescent yellow temple bulb splits into a thousand beams of rainbow colours. If *Ammi's* words are true, I am not a ravenous, egocentric and inconsiderate girl who serves selfish ends with familial sacrifices. I am a young woman rather, with a little heart that the world takes great pleasure in intimidating. Whenever he looks at me, his face lights up. If my mother's words are true, I am precious. I deserve to be cared for, to be loved beyond my body. I am everything he says I am.

"Everything, Adeeba—this temple, this city, this sky— everything is a sad story. There are just little streaks of happiness in between." He says, catching me unawares.

"Now, that is extremely poetic."

"My profound fondness for reading poetry has perks. I beg your pardon, love," he says. We chuckle.

"Do you read poetry too, Adeeba?"

"*Ah*…no. But my sister was a poetry person. She used to read sonnets from a poet called Maktub Ansari, and like a fanatic, I must say."

"That's exactly how I read Pablo Neruda!

> *…so I love you because I know no other way*
>
> *than this: where I does not exist, nor you,*
> *so close that your hand on my chest is my hand,*
> *so close that your eyes close as I fall asleep.*"

"Nice, now elaborate to me what you said."

"*Arghh!* You killed my Neruda mood."

"Neruda mood, *eh*? Explain now," I roll my eyes.

"When I was six, we had a trip to Paris. The four of us, we were standing at the top of the Eiffel tower, watching the city sparkle. In that moment, it felt like a family to me, the kind I had envied my friends for having."

"I am listening."

"So yes, I never felt like that again."

"But why do you hate your father?"

"Long story!"

"Shut up and tell me." He gave me a look and sighed.

"Look, Veer. It takes me just one glance to tell that something bothers you. This is not the first time you are choking at this point."

"…and just one glare to make me spill everything out."

"Yes, so please!" I ran my fingers through his hair and smiled.

"When we returned, my grandma was dead. I was only six then, so I don't remember much. *Didi* was nine, though.

She had passed away a week ago, but dad hadn't told me or *didi*. I had thought Paris was a family holiday, but it had been a business trip. A fucking business trip! My parents. They are not good parents. I mean, are they really even parents? I don't think so.

My father didn't even bother to treat us like his children. The arrogant, self-made billionaire! We were always his property, his assets. With fluctuating values. My horrible mother is an ideal wife who only speaks when and what dad asks her to.

They knew everything, Adeeba. Everything. They knew she was being molested, but they said nothing. Did nothing."

Maybe I have plucked the wrong string. All I can do is listen to him now.

"You know what they did to us, Adeeba, when we were children?"

"Hmm?"

"They abandoned us. They were too busy founding the 'Sood Empire'. They wanted to turn their family name into a brand.

All I remember from childhood is *didi* feeding me breakfast one morsel after another, grandma braiding her hair. Papa had an unsteady business then, so my parents made trips to several countries to pitch to investors. She wasn't ever in their *plan* (I wasn't either, but I was to be the heir to their to-be empire. So they were happy), you know, but why would they make it obvious to her? They made promises instead. After all, you don't have to keep them.

They loved her; they said so, always. Of course, they did not take her with them, wherever on earth they went.

They told her fancy stories about all those places when they called, which happened once every three-four weeks. My *didi* believed all of them. I wonder if they ever asked about me. It didn't matter. Maybe because I was too little to miss my absent parents, or maybe because *didi* had filled that gap for me. She was only three years elder to me, but she behaved like a mother. She would whip me with her skipping rope when she found unfinished *dal chawal* on my plate. She would also lay my head in her lap in the nights, and pass on the wisdom she had garnered over her eventful life of seven years.

She was grandma's favourite. She would tease me with that, but when it started upsetting me, she stopped. She would then whisper in my ears, "*Toh kya hua*, you are my favourite!"

So yes, I didn't miss them. *Didi* did however, a little too much. They brought her the fanciest toys from the most expensive shops in the world, but how could toys ever replace parents? She had a heap of never-played-with toys in one corner of her room.

Grandma was our solace. She fermented curd every day, because little Yukta *didi* loved to have *dahi chawal* for lunch. She also made the best pasta in the world for me. She never ridiculed *didi* for her failing grades in school, unlike maa-papa. She used to sit with her when she played her favourite piano piece—*London Bridge is falling*. Little Yukta *didi* used to be fascinated with music and musical instruments. She wanted to be the best pianist in the world. Maa-papa did not know of her dream. Grandma did.

She braided her hair and taught her to tie her shoelaces and polish her shoes. *Didi* always asked to be taught more. She wanted to learn every household work. As a seven-year-old, she could make a dough of flour, boil eggs, wash her own clothes, clean the bathroom and prepare scrambled eggs, tea and omelets.

When maa-papa were home, she did all of that so they would be pleased with her. She made tea for papa every afternoon and made the bed for maa every night. Every time she cooked something, she would run to show them, expecting they would be all happy and excited. They even reacted the same way, but it never convinced her.

Deep within, little Yukta *didi* harboured hope. When maa-papa saw she would not be a 'liability', they would take her along. Whenever she felt something against that, her naïve heart sank.

When she was seven, maa-papa came back. Papa had found an investor; the Sood chain of Hotels was at the top again. Just when she had managed to make peace with their absence, they had to return.

They were all excited to live with their children finally, but Yukta *didi* was not. Umpteen times she would start crying just like that. Maa-papa asked her what had happened, but she never had anything to say."

He breaks off, and silence falls upon us. I interlock his arm in mine and rest my head on his shoulder. His teary eyes shine.

"*Didi* was devastated when she returned from the trip. So maa-papa sold her the story that grandma had become a star. She was only nine, Adeeba. Only nine. She believed them this time even. She started reading about the sky, the stars, the galaxies, everything about space. She wouldn't sleep for nights, just read. She wanted to figure out a way to turn grandma back to human.

Until she grew up, and realized it couldn't happen."

"That's not all. I know," I say, almost in a whisper.

"I wish it was." He lets out a sigh.

"I want to say so much right now, but I am going to choke for the most part of it. *Shit!* What I am even saying…I don't know what I should say…but…"

"Adeeba! Adeeba…Adeeba…*shhhhh!* I know that. Why are you pressing it so hard upon yourself?"

"*Hmmm.*" He pulls out his arm from mine and wraps it tightly around me.

"Do what you do best. Listen."

"Yes!" I say. He lights another cigarette.

"Veer?"

"*Hmm?*"

"You said…*ah*…your sister…she was…"

"…molested. Yes."

"*Ummmm…*"

"Not today, Adeeba. *Mood off ho jayega mera.*"

"*Hmm.* Okay."

As silence falls, the distant city noises rise to surface. I have known from books and movies that dreams of love are often fragile. But in this moment, the air smells of cigarettes. There is a man who loves me, and a city beneath my feet, in a glass case perhaps, so its boisterous cacophony barely manages to whisper. No matter what happens of us, this moment will never be a lie.

"You know, Adeeba, when I was fourteen, I would sit at the terrace with Yukta *didi*. The profligate terrace of our mighty mansion, equipped with a swimming pool, a bar and a gym. We would just sit in a corner and gaze at the sky. Yukta *didi* has the names of stars, constellations and galaxies at her fingertips. She used to tell me many theories about space and parallel universes, of which I remember little, of course.

We knew grandma was not a star, but we had picked our favourite constellations. I would sit there for hours, explaining why mine was grandma, and hers was not. She always won, but okay.

Now that I think of it, it all makes sense. It's all a sad story," says Veer.

"What exactly is a sad story?" I ask.

"Everything, Adeeba. Everything is a sad story. There are just little streaks of happiness in between."

"This will need a lot of explanation."

"You see Adeeba, happiness is an eternal pursuit."

"I don't think so. Happiness is gratitude. Bow down to the things you have. What's not good enough for you is someone else's dream."

"Gratitude brings you satisfaction, but that is just one facet of happiness. The idea that many people starve for things that you have is real. It keeps you grounded, but it cannot contain your human aspect. Humans harbour dreams, and hunt them down within their capacity. But once they have it, they put it up in their showcases as *conquered*. It starts losing its lustre, the lustre that excites, the lustre that incites a drive to act. Then we get ourselves a new dream, a new thing to chase.

We all chase things we don't have. We all get our hearts broken in the process, but that doesn't mean we are not grateful for the things we do have."

"Like?"

"Like if I lose my company, my career, or say you, I will be devastated. But Yukta *didi* will still mean the same to me.

You know Adeeba, my whole teenage I wanted just one thing—to flee with *didi* from that hell my parents wanted us to believe was home. At twenty-six, I started a business venture, and within a year and a half, it was successful. I was a success.

I could now afford the freedom I so deeply desired, and I was sure I would never want anything beyond that. But was that true? No."

"*Hmmm.*"

"I am so happy right now, Adeeba," he whispers.

"The little moments of happiness are so underrated, no?" I say.

"Yes, they are the ones that make days bearable," he replies.

"You know, when I'm having a bad day, I paint. I have a room full of canvas sheets and artboards, everything I have ever painted."

"*Hmmm.* And why have I not been invited yet?"

"You earn your invitation to that room."

"*Achha!* He giggles; so do I. He stands up and dusts himself, after which he pulls me up. He holds my hand from behind, and makes me point above.

"Do you see those stars?" He says.

"Yes."

"They are the streaks of happiness. The underlying dark sky, the sad story, our lives. Do you know why you can see so many of them?" He asks.

"I might know. High altitude, reduced levels of pollution, so the light is not scattering," I reply.

"Yes, exactly. When you let yourself fill with dirt, you lose your stars. You forget how to create your streaks of happiness. Do you see some stars shine brighter than others?"

"Yes?"

"They are your dreams, passions and hobbies. The things you do just for yourself, and the little acts of kindness you commit to others. Now, there are those little dark spaces in between, you see?"

"They are not so little, actually. They are many light-years of distance," I object.

"Yes, but they look little. The more you zoom in, the larger they get. Those are our miseries," he explains.

"You are a philosopher!" I exclaim. He grins.

"Now follow my finger, and keep joining the dots in your head. Tell me what shape you see." He holds my hand again and starts pointing.

"*Umm*…I don't know. A parallelogram with a triangle projecting out at one vertex, maybe?"

"That is Lyra, a constellation. It is a fairly small constellation, but it includes the Vega, the fourth brightest star in the sky. They say it looks like a harp, but blah! *Mujhe bhi* parallelogram *hi lagta hai*."

"One more, Veer. Please. One more," I say, like a fangirl almost. He holds my hand again.

"It is…*ah*…a paper plane, with one wing slightly crumpled…maybe an arrow…I don't know. What is it?" I am confused.

"It is Aquila. An Eagle."

"An eagle? What? No way. How on earth does it look like an eagle?"

"It is difficult to recognize constellations if you do not know them beforehand. Do you see that star?" He says, pointing up. I nod.

"That's Altair. That's the brightest star in the constellation Aquila the Eagle. You know, Aquila is best known as the pet eagle of Zeus, the king of the Greek gods. It had the job of holding Zeus' lightning bolts…"

"That is too much information, seriously," I cut him. "But the constellations. Where do they fit in your metaphor?"

"Constellations, they are entities of stars. They are the people we love, the people who love us. You know, these constellations are not visible to you all the time. The earth rotates; they disappear, but they always stay in place, even when you cannot see them. And they always reappear, except when…"

"…When you let the dirt outside fill in and lose your stars. Yeah okay. Is that always true? I mean, sometimes you do nothing, and people just leave you."

"You are a star to them too, and they can lose you just the same way."

"It's so unfair."

"That it is. Note that they have dark spaces in between too." He says, at which I pause to ponder.

"See that star now," he asks again.

"Which one?"

"That." He makes me point. "That is the North Star, or the Pole Star—Polaris. It is famous for holding still while the entire northern sky moves around it. It is located at nearly the north celestial pole, the point about which the entire northern sky turns."

"Okay, but what does that represent?"

"That star…is you."

We pause and just breathe.

"These stars, they are so beautiful," I say.

"Not as beautiful as you, Adeeba."

"*Yaar! Chup karo.*"

"What? I can call my girlfriend beautiful!"

"Stop it, Veer."

"Why always, Adeeba?"

"I just hate that word. That compliment."

"But why, what's wrong?"

"I just don't like that thing…compliment. What is my achievement if I am beautiful?"

"What are you saying, Adeeba!"

"Nothing, just stop."

"Okay."

4

"A deeba *didi,* you're so old, but you still pee in bed. *He hee he!*" A patch of the bedsheet beside Bhoomi is wet. Her frock is too. I had checked her at night, so she must have done this in the morning. Of course, she has done that! She will not remember it, though. I rush to the kitchen and put a *bhagona* full of water on the stove. With lukewarm water, I wash her feet. I pull out a frock from the closet and ask her to change her clothes, but she does not know why.

"Why change clothes, *beta?* And do you expect your mother to wear a frock? Where is your *burkha?* What is wrong with you? Wait, why am I wearing a frock already, and why is it wet?" She becomes all puzzled again, just like every other time.

"*Ammi,* you only said last night frocks were more comfortable to sleep in. Don't stress so much, change your clothes, and go brush your teeth. It's a fine morning."

"Yeah, okay!"

She goes into the bathroom to freshen up. As I press my face against the mesh of my window, a dandelion seed lands on my upper lip. I blow it off, but its milky white hairy bristles leave a ticklish imprint.

I remember the day I saw her for the first time. I was nine then. It was a fine morning, just like this one. She was new to the school, or the village for that matter. *Ammi* had told me her parents lived there nine years ago. After she was born, they had shifted to her *nani's* place for some time. We had made friends on the first day of school.

Boys hit on her, for she was beautiful. She is beautiful. In no time, she had become my best friend. Ours was a government school, four hours from our village, in the nearest town, Mahabaleshwar. We both loved school. We both hated boys.

She had a silly habit of losing stationary all the time. So I carried an extra set to school. Whenever she lost something (which she did every second or third day), she turned to me for help. Every time I handed her what she needed, I tapped on her head gently, smiling at her frivolousness.

Back then, I believed in Allah. Infatuation, to me, was a filthy concept, but I was safe. I was not drooling over boys; I hated most of them instead. The only thing two young girls could share was friendship. This friendship, however, was more pleasant than others. "What would you do without me?" I would say, and we chuckled. The very thought of it made my heart take a leap of faith, and the butterflies inside me caught it safely as it descended.

I loved saying it so much that sometimes I craved for her to lose something. Once it so happened, she went for days without asking for a pencil. I waited, waited and waited, but she did not lose anything. My restlessness peaked.

The day we had our Mathematics exam, I managed to pilfer her eraser. I closed my fist tight so she could not see it. When she was scavenging her bag for the essentials outside the examination hall, she realized something was missing. The look on her face changed.

And there I was, at her rescue, my fist pressed against my back, pretending I knew nothing of her situation.

"All the best!" I said.

"Adeeba…*ah*, actually, I don't have an eraser. Can you lend me one?"

Just then, the invigilator asked everyone to hurry up. I opened my fist to her. She picked the eraser and rushed in without realizing it was her own.

When the test was over, she came running to me. She hugged me so tight I felt her heart thump.

"Thank you so much, Adeeba. You saved me today."

"What would you do without me!" I tapped on her head.

"Die of panic attacks possibly," she said, and we chuckled. With that, we parted ways.

I must have been smiling then.

On my way back home, I took the longer route, though. I went to the mosque where *Maulvi Sahab* used to sit. When I was younger, *Ammi* took Sabeena and me to this mosque, which she believed was the perfect place to confess one's sins to Allah.

The first time I had confessed something, I had done so out loud with my eyes closed, only to realize that he had heard everything. He had come to me with a black feather and a light, wooden box.

"You see this feather. All our sins weigh just as much as this feather to Allah. When kept in this box, they add negligibly to its weight. He can forgive all of them, given you confess. If you don't, they add up, and the box starts weighing because of them."

Ever since then, I had made all my confessions to him. He would listen to me like no one else did. That afternoon, I sat with him and confessed my theft.

"Allah will forgive you."

"*Astaghfirullah*," I had said.

Vehicles honked to break my train of thoughts. There was a traffic jam in front of me. The sun was up, and the city was through with day business. More importantly, Bhoomi had bathed, and my family was up for breakfast.

Bhoomi could not make new memories anymore. She did remember things from her former life, though. Except that I was the only thing from her *former life* that was still relevant. Her brain could not store anything anymore, so she forgot everything after fifteen minutes. She was a case of Anterograde Amnesia.

Anterograde Amnesia is a mental condition, which happens when there is an injury to a part of the brain called hippocampus. That was what the doctors had told me. Bhoomi could learn new skills, though. You can say Bhoomi could learn how to ride a bicycle, but she would not remember learning it…just like she remembered my face, but forgot who I was to her, always. Her brain made something up every time. Sometimes she was my mother, sometimes my little sister, sometimes the elder one. Every fifteen minutes, she and I had a new connection. I never told her the truth. To end this lesbian woman's love story—I loved her, and she loved me back in a hundred different ways.

It had happened to her twelve years ago when she was seventeen. A massive blow with a rod at the back of her head. Everyone's life had changed…forever.

5

Sabeena was only five when *Abbu* had died of kidney failure. *Ammi* did not have the money to perform the last rites, even book a spot to bury his body. The *chachas* and *taus* took care of that—the beauty of villages. *Ammi* became the breadwinner of the family. She was only twenty-four then, young and desirable enough to have to kick away several *nikaah* proposals.

In beauty, everyone said I was her *parchai* (shadow). Beauty, *huh*—it can curse a woman just as much as it can bless. Men like to smell and adore and cherish it, but also derive pleasure from crushing it.

Ammi did not fear men, though. She had only trusted one man in her life—the man she had loved, *Abbu*. The rest had only ever received scepticism from her. Although swirling them around could have been a cakewalk, *Ammi* chose ethics and Allah's commandments.

And my *Ammi* could fight them. That is where, the villagers said, Sabeena had gotten her flair for picking up fights from. We were the two halves of *Ammi*—me her beauty, Sabeena her valour.

After *Abbu* was gone, *Ammi* had to take up physical labour. She joined a contractor who hired labourers for construction sites. But she was a woman—half the normal wages, work only where surplus is needed. For us, though, it was enough.

In her free afternoons, when she was home, we would have our little family time—her *champee,* stories with life lessons and the touch of her profound wisdom, Sabeena's rants, lunch together. On the days she was at work, Sabeena would be my responsibility.

After *Abbu's* demise, the tension of fending for two daughters had consumed my mother. In the evenings, I opened the door to a knackered and cranky *Ammi*. On most days, I would be the one cooking dinner, for *Ammi* pulled off late shifts. Sabeena would be asleep by the time she arrived. There were dark circles beneath her eyes, and fringes of grey hair above her ears, which she now wore a *hijab* to hide. *Ammi's* beauty was fading.

For almost twelve years, I had raised Sabeena. I had protected her from the storms that had ravaged *Ammi* and me. In all fairness, I was her second mother.

My far-fetched musings lingered over a thought sometimes. Even when I was a woman, a mother to my own bearings, Sabeena would remain my first child. My fingertips traced her face—her forehead, down her right cheek, all the way to her chin. I would pass my finger carefully over the bump of her mole. Her skin, tawny, scabrous. Her nose, pierced on the right. A scar on her left cheek.

At five, she had incurred that scar. Girls and women of Rohila could not go to cemeteries and graveyards, but Sabeena was a child. When the men lifted *Abbu's* coffin and started their march, Sabeena ran after them. She stumbled and fell flat upon a stone. Her cheek hit its pointed end.

Sabeena had not stopped wailing for two days straight. I had wept with her, only that my concerns extended beyond her pain. She had stitches on her face, and unlike Sabeena, *Ammi* and I knew what that could mean to a girl. Everyone in the village said Sabeena was young. The scar would go as she aged.

Five years later, it was still there, as much an eyesore as ever. I knew it was one of her deepest insecurities.

And I knew how her insecurities triggered her to function. She did not wear a *hijab*. She always stressed that physical beauty was a horrible metric for acceptance. She was the messiah to every girl. Fighting boys was like an addiction to her.

If you think my little sister's complex stood on a noxious premise, let me stop you there. If you think I should not have let Sabeena's delicate young years be consumed by that insecurity, let me tell you something.

Beauty does wonders for you while it lasts. If only I could fairly explain what being beautiful is to a woman!

One of my favourite stories from *Baba* is that of the creation of women. When the Hindu god *Brahma* created the world with his mind, he populated it with beings which could self-fertilize. According to his master plan, these beings would create children from within themselves, look after them until they were six, and then perish. No chaos whatsoever.

When these beings came into existence, though, *Brahma* realized they were all men. His artistic mastery had failed to manifest a woman. That's where Lord *Shiva*, the god of destruction and husband to mother earth, came into the picture. He pulled out a woman from *Brahma's* mind—*Brahma's* mind-born daughter. He then explained to him about men, women and the ecstasy of coming together.

But *Brahma* was not listening. He had taken one look at his mind born daughter and decided he wanted her. *Shiva* sat there, watching the great father lusting for his own daughter, chasing her all over the cosmos because he wanted to possess her.

What a sin I have brought into this world!

To fix what he had done, he castrated himself, merged with his own wife, and presented himself to *Brahma*. But *Brahma*, by now, had experienced the frenzy of union. So he pried apart *Shiva* from his wife, and said,

"From now on, men and women will be born as separate entities. They shall live as separate entities and populate my world through the joy of coming together." He created a race of men and a race of women on the earth, but nothing happened. Nobody knew what to do.

Shiva came to the rescue again. "Tickle each other," he said to these men and women. "The rest shall follow."

The story ends here, but think a little deeper now. When I told you of Brahma's mind born daughter, what picture did you paint of her in your mind—a creature with ethereal beauty or a disfigured, obese body with speckles and scars all over, housing an ordinary soul?

When *Brahma's* men and women populated this earth, they formed tribes. Be it primitive hunter gatherers or sophisticated civilians, we know from history, all tribes were male driven. The ones who could fight became warriors. The visionary warriors became emperors. And the lower strata of the society comprised men who were neither valiant nor visionaries.

When *Shiva* asked these men to tickle women, who would the strongest and the most competent men have wanted to tickle? Pretty women, or the not so pretty ones? Who, amidst the women, wielded more power—the former, or the latter?

In Rohila, if you were beautiful, you were more likely to be deemed fit by a man for marriage. If you were your *shauhar's* first wife, he would probably never marry again. If he already had wives, you would be the superior wife. You would have the control of the house and could dictate terms. You could choose how many children you wanted to have, whether you wanted to have one or not.

Now you know why the girls in the village, who Sabeena thought she led, liked her so much. They did not have to compete with her. That also explains why they did not like me.

In all the nights she gave way to her insecurities, she would grip me tight across my belly, and say, "Adeeba *Appi*, you are so beautiful. I love you." She would sigh then, and I wondered how many times she had seen reflected in the eyes of numerous people her very own scar, how many times she had told herself she was not beautiful. But I looked at her like a mother. To me, she was the prettiest girl in the world, even prettier than I was. I wanted to tell her that, but I always choked. How could I expect of her that it be enough?

Pressing her against my chest, in whispers, so *Ammi* did not wake up, I would sing to her my lullaby.

> *The fairy with that speck on her face,*
> *Must smile like the moon with its dark craters shines.*
> *Smile and smile till she falls asleep…*
> *Smile and smile till…she falls…asleep.*

In the village, if only you could see how boys behaved around me! The reckless, rusty and rogue boys who would extract extreme sacrifices from their *bibis,* would don their most charming, compassionate and far from misbehaved conduct. They spoke with sensitivity, vulnerability and utmost respect for women. The ones who would treat me, or any woman for that matter, with love, care and esteem, who would make good *shauhars,* would shy away from me. If by any chance, we crossed paths, they looked down. Sweat flushed their foreheads. Their hands shivered and feet trembled, as they walked past me with fastened strides.

Those very reckless, misbehaved boys hit my little sister right where it hurt. They called her *Nishanwali,* the girl with a scar. Those were the boys Sabeena used to fight with the most. Sabeena laughed at how they stepped back and shied from me when I tried to resolve the fights. "Why are you quiet now? Speak *na,* whatever the hell you were saying about me. *Appi* is here, that's why? *Haha!*"

The child that she was, she thought they feared my confrontation, the way she did. She thought my glare had an authority, which was true, except that it was not. The boys would say, "yeah, that is exactly why. Your *Appi* does not like words much. If only I knew what she likes, besides you, *Nishanwali!* I swear on god; I would do that right now." They gave sly smiles to each other, and to me. It infuriated Sabeena as much as it confused.

I would be lying if I say I do not spend my leisure hours pondering over their admirations with contemptuous pity. Back then I did not know the origin of my apathy for those boys. But a decade later, having worked as a tourist guide for so many years, I think I do.

You may call it guilty pleasure, but I liked resolving fights for Sabeena. Girls like admiration, even from boys they love to hate. Our maidenly modesty does not allow us to admit that. Although, what is modesty? The mesh that civilizations have woven for themselves to curb individuals from setting themselves free? Till how far can it follow you? It ceases to exist when you are away from the people who practise it. It changes with demography, religion and culture. The familiar faces, the sense of belongingness to a society imposes rules on you. The people who know you expect you to behave in a certain way. With strangers, you are free.

When Sabeena walked with me in the streets, people looked at us differently. In the eyes of the maidens, I saw jealously for me. The women and elderly people believed *Ammi* was blessed, for my marriage would be much less a liability for her.

The boys shot glances at me. Boys of my age, boys younger or older than me, and sometimes even men who would smoke *bidis* and discuss politics with *Abbu* if he were alive. They smiled at me—nervous, sly, flirtatious, sometimes even scary smiles. A few reckless boys even adjusted their crotch when they saw me. I had been followed quite a few times, but they had never crossed the line. I would pretend none of this had ever happened, but I will not lie; it did feel good. For me, their eyes had awe, infatuation and even lust. I could sway them if and as I pleased. *Astaghfirullah*, but that was power.

In the same eyes, for Sabeena, I had seen remorse, pity, indifference, or worse, ridicule. The misbehaved boys hit her right where it hurt. The decent boys were pitiful, as if they wanted to apologize to her, for they could not see themselves with her in love or marriage. To the elderly, she was the *noor* of their eyes, but if only that could compensate!

My little sister envied me. In years to come she would grow vindictive. It hurt me; I loved her. When I looked at myself through her eyes though, I saw Adeeba wielding a power Sabeena could never possess.

6

A musty odour lurks in the air. Jammed from days of not opening, the window glass gives a shattering blare as I jerk it open. The sun barges into the little room I like to call my art gallery.

My fingers run upon the leniently textured sheet taped to the artboard, layered with neutral grey acrylic primer. The bristles of my brush lace with colours as I mix them to prepare the different skin tones I need. My colleagues like to believe I am a miser. I give them that—I have a family to feed. My art is the only thing I spend like a brat on.

I draw the outline of his face; I start with his eyes. The pallet is ready; I have my brushes and media in place. The room is well-ventilated to avoid toxicity. I am all set to paint Veer's portrait.

What are we, if not these shades of mixed colours— blends of burnt umber, ultramarine blue, cadmium red, titanium white—every composition unique, endless possibilities. We have our fair share of black too. We are all a collection of nuances.

Yet the world shuffles between dichotomies. You can either be a man or a woman; you have little choice with that. If you are a man, you can only love a woman. You must woo her, put up a fight. If you are a woman, well, you must wait till a man makes the first move. You are immodest otherwise. You must dress accordingly, behave in a certain way. The list never ends.

Are we not all rainbows, though, hiding most of our colours, so the world sees only one? What about men who love men, or women who love women? If to love is to lose control, why should it follow pre-set rules? Why should the outliers be decreed to a miserable life?

The afternoon I turned sixteen, Bhoomi had planned a *kairi* treat for me, for us. After school, I followed her lead to *Phadnis chacha's* garden. The moment I stepped in, I knew she wanted his infamously agonising stick on her back. But cunning as she was, she talked the guards into believing we were *chacha's* nieces. For good one hour, we kept savouring the tart *kairis,* laughing at our little act of anarchy.

Then she looked into my eyes. My stomach churned with euphoria. The dead yellow leaves munched under our feet. I did not know when or how, but we drew close. I leaned towards her, our fingers interlocked. As my lips fused into hers, my body heated up like a furnace. She sucked on my upper lip; I bit her lower. Blood spurted out of her lip; it was tastier than juice. In that moment, a million ecstatic outbursts were happening within me. I groped her breasts, and she touched me between my legs. After one good minute, she withdrew. She started running, blushing as she did. I trailed after her.

With every footstep, though, we walked into a world that would despise us now. Beyond that sky, there was a god we had betrayed, in our heads, shreds of a broken promise we had made to him in prayers. That afternoon, I took the longer route, again.

In the mosque, I closed my eyes and confessed to Allah, this time secretly.

"He won't forgive you…" said *Maulvi Sahab*. My heart thudded.

"…unless you are repentant," he completed.

I opened my eyes. A question catapulted me into an existential crisis—was I even sorry?

7

My sinuses hurt from the oil media odour as I paint the big spots with thick, rough strokes—burnt umber and some thinner for the hair, raw umber to stain the eyes. I then darken the pupils and outline the nose and the lips with fine bristles. A touch of burnt sienna gives warmth to his eyes.

When the first layer of colours dries, I start working on the facial details—the construction of the head, the values of colours, the highlights, mid-tones and shadows. For contrast, I add some warm halftones to the face, against cold bluish halftones to the background. A blend of white and ultramarine blue for the sclera, a detailing with burnt sienna to the pupils. A touch of bluish white makes them glossy—Veer's face starts taking form.

Thirteen years ago, I kissed Bhoomi. My identity has been a messy labyrinth ever since. The rush of feelings I felt for Bhoomi, I have never felt for another woman. As for men, I rarely find ones who tour round the city with me without lusting. Ones who will not try to grab my booty, grope my breasts or pin me against a wall in some isolated pocket in the city. The organisation will not let us say no to clients, even though one look is enough to understand misplaced intentions.

But one day I see a man, and everything starts changing.

One of my tourists wanted to do a hot air balloon ride. As the basket took off, I stood below waving at her. Unlike most other balloons in the sky, this one was not local. It had cleaner equipment, a more aesthetic basket with a huge logo, *WanderHeist.*

At my vision's periphery, a man stood at the air station a few yards away. His fine black suit hung beautifully over a six feet tall, gym-built body. All the weight on his right leg, left leg free and bent, hands in the pockets, as if posing for a photograph. People around him had tablets in their hands, and were tallying something with the local air service in charge.

My client had had a tough time arguing why that particular balloon cost five hundred bucks more than the others. She had to settle with the answer that it belonged to that man. His company, *WanderHeist,* was one of the largest adventure-sport franchises in the country. They provided better equipped and much safer rides.

All the commotion around was not enough to dissuade me from his perpetually staring hazel eyes. Yet, my guards were not up. His simplicity tore through the aura of sophistication he was wearing. He smiled at me the way you smile at a flower you want to adore and not pluck.

I visited that place multiple times a day, with different tourists, and I would see him at least once every day. I wondered how his timing could be such a coincidence—he was a busy man. He would stand just the same way, not too far and never too close. We did exchange glances sometimes, always by chance, I swear. Every time it happened, something gnawed inside me—a man I knew nothing about was stalking me, and I was…beginning to like it.

I wanted my life to pause there. If it continued to flow, it would take one of the two courses—I could either never discover who I was, or unleash something I could never come to terms with.

It went on like that for umpteen days, until one evening, he walked up to me and extended his hand.

"Hi, I am Veer. Do you mind if I drop you home?"

I am almost done. I smoothen the stroke edges and adjust the shadows to include a light source. When done, the painting comes alive. I place the artboard amidst the only other portraits I have ever painted—the people that have been my family. *Ammi, Baba,* Sabeena, Bhoomi, and now Veer.

Veer had left his parents after his business boomed. Most cities in the country would have made better homes for him, but he chose my city. I am so grateful his sister wanted a serene home in the mountains. He cheers for her from amidst the audience when she plays the piano. Every month he celebrates her paycheck from a restaurant he can very conveniently acquire.

What I feel for him is pure, platonic love; I say that to myself every day. Although, how much of it is true?

For the greater part of my life, I have always been in-charge—of Sabeena, of the house when *Ammi* was at work, now of *Baba* and Bhoomi, of running our home. I have always taken the world upfront, be it solving fights for Sabeena, or dealing with douches in the name of tourists. Here was a man who gave me hugs and ice-creams when I needed, a man who wanted to solve every problem before it could cause as much as a wrinkle on my forehead. A man who would not, because he respected me enough to stand aside and let me fight my own battles.

My Veer is adorable. He texts me every night, and mostly does not have anything to say, except for *how was your day*. When we go for days without talking, it exasperates him. And he has this innocent paranoia of losing me—to time, to distance, to not talking for two days in a row, and what not. Filled with explosive thoughts, he calls me and says,

"Adeeba, why do you never call me?"

Why do I never text him first? Don't I feel like talking too, just the way he does…so on. He writes all his volatile impulses in texts in the middle of the night, then deletes them before I read. *I can't hurt you with words I will not mean just minutes later.* For what it's worth, all this vulnerability comes from a man who signs deals with top class executives every day, a man with a vision for his company, a condescending voice, and a work ethic which commands respect at every table he sits.

He wants to know everything about me, from my little whims and fancies, to *Baba's* morning errands and the best ways to make friends with Bhoomi. He remembers all the petty things I tell him. *I haven't met anyone in your life. I already feel very distant, and you never make it any easy,* he says, all the time.

The other day we sat at that temple again. He pulled out a folded sheet of yellow, almost brittle paper.

"I found this poet, Adeeba. Maktub Ansari."

"Oh god! Veer, why?" I chuckled.

"*Arre!* I wanted to read his work."

"Of course not!" My words coalesced with the chuckle into a laughter.

"Hey! *Huh*, whatever. I found his book of sonnets. He writes too much Islamic philosophy. Staunchly religious, very puritanical."

"*Hmm.* I see," I said, still laughing.

"Adeeba, please stop *yaar.*"

"Okay…okay! *Shhhhh!*" He placed his finger on my lips.

"Now shut up and listen to me. I found this very beautiful sonnet, and…"

"…and?"

"Nothing, *tum rehne do.*"

"And it reminded you of me?" I burst into laughter again. He stole his gaze.

"*Achha* sorry. I will be quiet now."

"*Nahi, tum rehne hi do ab.*"

"Veer, I won't laugh, promise."

"Okay."

"Show me that now," I said. He opened the folds; he had underlined something.

"This particular line Adeeba. It's my favourite.

> *My love, you are a perfect disarray,*
> *of jumbled footprints only I can trace.*
> *Sometimes a tailor…*"

"Veer, stop please."

"Not now, Adeeba. This next line is…"

"Please Veer, not this poem. Just not this." A memory was tearing through years of burial in my head.

"*Arre!* At least listen to it once *na…*"

"Veer please! Not this one."

8

Things changed when Sabeena hit thirteen.

The fissured mirror in the bathroom, with water stains sprinkled all over like polka dots, became her best friend. On the streets, she wrapped her *dupatta* around her head in the way of *hijab*, never failing to drape the loose end of it over her scar. Her strides transitioned into mincing maidenly footsteps, and her fights with boys dropped in both frequency and volatility as if she had stopped hating them. She also started bleeding every month.

When Sabeena had bled for the first time, *Ammi* was not at home. It was a December afternoon. She was bathing when she noticed blood beneath her toes, mixing with water, losing its consistency as it flowed towards the sink. A thin red stream channeled down her calves, down her knees, her thighs, vagina. It terrified her so much she started screaming. She drenched me all over with a tight hug. Her lower abdomen started cramping as if someone was twisting and crumpling her uterus; the panic only intensified it. A petrified Sabeena began to wail.

I wrapped her in a towel and rushed to the stove. With warm water, I made a polythene sack to put on her belly. In minutes, the pain retreated from her body like a defeated army.

"*Appi*, you saved me today," Sabeena said, in a heartfelt tone.

"Sabeena, nothing would happen to you even if I were not here," I said, smiling, as I soaked her wet hair dry in a hand towel. She lay on the cot, wrapped in a towel from breasts to knees.

"*Matlab?*" (Meaning)

"This will happen for a day or two every month, Sabeena."

"But why *Appi?*"

"Because you are a woman now."

"I am only 13, *Appi?*"

"Yes, that's when you become a woman, *beta.*"

"And that means I should endure this pain, and bleed? Why would *Allah taala* do this to women?"

"Don't say that Sabeena. Allah has given us women a beautiful capability—we can bear lives. He tests us every month to befit us for that."

"This will never stop?"

"It will, *beta*. When you grow old."

Sabeena was overwhelmed, frightened at the thought; so I held her tight against my side and caressed her cheek. It worked for Sabeena all the time.

"You will get used to it. You are my strong girl."

"Woman. *Khikhikhi…*" Her teeth tore through her lips as she chuckled.

Sabeena had ceased to be an *Adeeba Appi fanatic*. She did not stroll after me in the streets or interlocked the colour pencils between her fingers when I painted. She had even started retaliating to my angry words. She dressed for school and managed all her homework by herself. She had also stopped fighting boys. Lastly, her behaviour at school had absorbed the maidenly modesty all girls around her encompassed.

I missed all the things about her that irritated me.

Although, if I had lost a fan in Sabeena, I had found one in Bhoomi. Even our mothers wanted us together. Bhoomi's *Aai* always bought an extra half kilo of *kalakand* for Diwali because I loved them. And though Bhoomi's family did not eat meat, they would let her celebrate Bakrid with *Ammi* and Sabeena. We were inseparable. '*Adeeba kuthe ahe* (where is Adeeba),' whenever someone asked, the other always replied, '*Bhoomiasathi disate. Apana tila sapadela.* (Look for Bhoomi. You will find her.)'

We loved that about us. We did not know who we were to each other; we had sworn to ourselves we would never try to find out.

Rohila lay on the outskirts of Mahabaleshwar. For all kids in our village, the only accessible school was Marutirao Puran School on the city's outskirts. Our bus to school left at five sharp. Sabeena would hold my index finger as we walked to the stop, though she was almost my height. That would be one time of the day when she behaved like my little Sabeena.

She had lately taken a liking to books, particularly poetry. Typically, my sister. And since she had a hurricane of hormones inside her, love and depression were the favourite food for her thoughts. At the back of our school, there was a flea-market where they sold old books at dirt-cheap prices. Sabeena would clutch my hand as I walked her through a crowded concourse of people rubbing against each other, sweating in the summer heat. Our mouths tasted of dust rising from footsteps beating against the ground; our nostrils burst from it. We would miss our bus on the days we had some fortune collected over months to spend on weary books with brittle brown pages, loose bindings and broken spines. We walked back ten kilometres to home, hopping with joy, celebrating our books and bragging about the bargains.

One such afternoon, Sabeena's gaze caught a thin, dilapidated book of sonnets by a poet called Maktub Ansari, fallen off a pile of rusty hardcovers. Sabeena had some change left after buying a book, so she dived into a hard bargain with the vendor. And nobody bargained better than my sister. We did not know if we would ever read it, but the sheer pleasure of having bought two books when we were head over heels for just one was too much to take.

The next morning, Sabeena came running to me with that book. She opened it at the dog-eared page, and asked me to read a poem.

> You are a scorching summer's petrichor,
> an icy wind of winter afternoon.
> A pensive poet's musings' paramour,
> the lurking love he sees behind the moon.
> My love, you are a perfect disarray,
> of jumbled footprints only I can trace—
> sometimes a tailor-made woman's essay;
> sometimes a girl with naïve, holy grace.
> The thumping of your heart against my chest,
> your mellow snoring breath when you're asleep,
> I know so well can't be at mortal hest.
> You are so much your body cannot keep.
>
> So when I hold you close, I let you fly.
> So when I kiss your lips, I close my eyes.

"*Appi*, what does *paramour* mean?" She asked.

"It means a lover, someone you should not be involved with, outside marriage maybe. But why are you reading such sonnets, Sabeena?"

"I don't know *Appi*. I mostly don't understand any of these, but I like the rhythm, the words, the rhyme, the feel, everything."

"*Hmm*. The rhythm is nice indeed. The iambic pentameter is perfect."

"Wha…what? Iamb …ic what?"

"*Arre!* Iambic pentameter. A kind of meter which sonnets usually use. Every line has ten syllables…and…"

"*No…Appi…nahi yaar*. No lectures today. Explain to me the meaning of this sonnet."

"Okay, I will tell you roughly."

"Perfect!"

"This poet is one hell of a hopeless romantic. He starts with comparing her lover to the pleasant feelings like the smell of the first rain on hot soil. Also to unpleasant ones like a cold wind in winter. Meaning she is not perfect in any way.

He says that his lover is so full of life, her soul will always transcend her body. Therefore, he despises any metrics her body sets for her."

"*Appi*, you are a master at words, but why do you forget I am not? What does *transcend* mean? And *metric* and *despises*?"

"*Arre!*" I chuckled. "Simply put, it means your body cannot define who you are. So I love your soul."

"*Hmm!*"

"*Hmm!*"

"*Appi*, I love the last two lines,"

"Yes, yes, Sabeena. Me too!"

She took the book from my hand and walked away. There was a charm in her eyes, a belief, a hope. As young people, we believe one day we will find love, and that will fix everything. They will accept us for who we are and that alone will make everything easy. What more shall we need to be happy forever?

Her mind was weaving the same fairy tale that mine did when I was thirteen. But how do you save yourself from a reality that runs on different rules? What happens of fragile dreams when life hits?

The way boys looked at her, I knew her heart was going to break. How could I save my little sister from that?

9

The ghee, incense sticks and lotus aroma filled the fuggy, dim room. It was Tuesday, so there was a long queue outside, waiting to offer a jar of milk to the *Shivling*. Rumours had it that there used to be a shop there about thirty years ago. The *Shivling* tore through the earth; the devotees dismantled the shop. The Vashishtha Temple administration took over.

After almost an hour of tiring ourselves in the queue, Veer managed to reach the door. He handed the *prasad* to the *pandit*, who did him *tika* and returned the box along with a few petals of jimsonweed. As he emptied his cane over the slimy *Shivling,* splashes of milk appeared as white beads all over his jeans.

When he was done, we got out of that room. It was a summer afternoon; the sun was somewhere between pleasant and hot. The temple was full of people entering various rooms to visit different gods or waiting outside the hot water spring to bathe. It goes without saying that our favourite spot was occupied, so we decided to stroll in the streets of Manali.

As we walked down the stairs, he slid his fingers between mine. City noises meddled in our conversation; we had to raise our voices.

"Are you regular at temples, or is it to impress me?"

"*Hmm.* If I knew how to impress you, wouldn't I have already?" He chuckled, as a motorbike whizzed past us.

"Good point." I laughed too.

"Although, how much do I need to impress you? Given, you're my girl already."

"*Ohhho!* Your girl! *Hmmmmmmmm.*"

"*Huh?*" He rolled his eyes at me.

"You believe in all this?" I asked.

"What all this?"

"Temples, worshipping, gods, religion, its rules?"

"*Didi* does; she insists that I do too."

"Do you?"

"Not every god! Not so much in religion. I mean, I don't do *puja* all the time. I don't believe in most of the myths, traditions and shit. But I like to visit temples once in a while. Temples are calm and peaceful."

"*Hmmm.*"

"You know, as a kid, my favourite god was Hanuman, and Ganesha, because they were notorious and powerful…"

"…and had animated movies after them." I completed.

"*Hehehe* yes!"

"Who was your favourite god, Adeeba?"

"I have only one god—Allah, and I don't believe in him."

"What? You're Muslim? What is your full name?"

"Adeeba Sheikh." I did expect his demeanour to change, but it did not.

"Okay, but why don't you believe in your god?"

"Why do *you* believe in a god?"

"Because I want to believe there is a superior force that will guide me, protect me when I am in trouble, and can destroy me; so I need to fear. You see, Adeeba, faith is important. Without faith, without belief, our own selves will be too much for us to handle."

"*Hmmm.*"

"*Kya hmmm?*"

"I don't know, Veer. All that you say is fine, but how do I believe in a god who denies my existence."

"*Ummmm…*"

"There is nothing to hide from you, but I don't want to talk about it, or *mera mood kharaab ho jayega.*"

"It's okay, Adeeba. Let's get you an ice cream."

"Yes, please," I grinned, clutching his hand tighter.

He walked me into an aesthetic café—teenagers, English songs, sofas hanging from the ceiling to make fancy seats and torn novels as decoration on walls with artistic calligraphy. In one corner of the café, there was a small stage setup. On the elevated platform lay a full-size piano with its flap closed, a guitar resting on a stand, and a mic. A whiteboard read, *Music starts at 7 P.M.*

"My *didi* plays here, every evening," said Veer, as he handed me my *Cornetto.*

"The ambience is so nice."

"*Ah!* Wait till you hear her play. She makes this place bliss. The sales whoop when she plays."

"I can only ever doubt that. She's *your* sister, after all."

"Yes," he grinned. "Everyone loves her."

As we licked on our cones, we started walking back to the temple without notice. A lot of time had passed. It was five now; the sun, only an hour away from the horizon, had changed colour. The sky was a playground of raging crimson clouds with yellow fissures in between.

"Veer?"

"*Hmm?*"

"Why do you hate your father?"

"Long story, Adeeba."

"We have all the time."

"*Hmm.*"

"*Hmm kya*, say *na*!" He did not say anything.

"Veer, you always choke when you talk of your father. There is something that's hurting you. Tell me."

"Adeeba…"

"Okay, never mind." We walked in silence for good five minutes before he broke it.

"What do you I tell you, Adeeba—that my rich ass father let one of his bastard investors molest my sister for five months, so he could become richer?"

"Wha…what? He did what?"

"That man used to come home all suited and jolly, with gifts for *didi* and me. Around him, papa's attitude towards *didi* would change completely. He would be all praises for her. The man would pat *didi* at every compliment papa threw. Then he would ask her to play the piano for him. 'Yukta, take uncle to your room, *beta*,' he would say to a fifteen-year-old. Can you believe that?"

The temple was empty now; our favourite spot was free. We took our seats, and Veer continued.

"One evening, I wanted pencil colours from *didi*'s room. The door was barely open. *Didi* was playing the piano, but her ever-steady hands were shivering. The man stood behind her chair. His thumbs massaged the back of her neck, his other fingers beneath her *kurti*, directed towards her breasts…descending.

Tears dripped from her eyelashes; I could hear her sobs. I don't know what happened to me. I wanted to barge in and beat that man to pulp, but my legs had frozen. My hands were frozen. I couldn't move. Perhaps, that is how bad touch operates—it cripples your ability to fight.

I kicked the door hard; he withdrew. But as the door opened, I started shivering. My legs felt weak, my hands invalid. I was only twelve. I had never felt so frightened.

Didi ran to her room. I faced the man, who walked past me as if nothing had happened."

Veer was sniffing. His teeth clattered, his fists tight. I interlocked his arm in mine; I did not know how else to comfort him.

"In her room, she sat doubled up, her face shoved between her knees. I sat at her feet, but she wouldn't talk to me. '*Didi*, say something,' I broke into a flood of tears. She was weeping too, but she wouldn't look up. 'Did uncle beat you *didi*? What did he do?' She wouldn't say a thing. '*Didi*! *Didi*!'

I didn't know what that man had done; I was only twelve, Adeeba. I knew what rape was, but…I don't know. We reserve the most beautiful and the most terrible extremes for movies and or news channels; we expect life to happen somewhere in between. So when something hits us, we don't know how to react. We turn our faces so we don't have to confront it."

"But you confronted it, Veer. You moved out of that place."

"No, I moved out because it became unbearable. *Didi* didn't let me talk to my parents, not when I was twelve, not when I was sixteen, or eighteen, or twenty."

"But why?"

"She wanted to protect me. Do hell with that protection if I could not fight for her." He broke off.

"It happened again, and again, Adeeba. *Didi* used to weep in front of me, but she never told me what had happened. She wouldn't let me talk to maa-papa too. So I just wept with her."

I caught sight of a little boy, four or five years old, looking back at us as his limping mother adjusted her walking stick on the stairs to walk down. I did not know… he had Sabeena's eyes.

"That man's visits stopped. Years passed; I grew up. I understood by myself what my sister had gone through. I couldn't even bring myself to look at my parents as parents after that, Adeeba!"

"Veer, they didn't know that. For them, he was just an investor. Why…"

"They did, Adeeba!" He almost screamed. A tear trickled down his cheek.

"How do you know?"

"Papa still calls me up sometimes, purging me to come back *home*. His *grand empire* would be heirless otherwise, *na*! That night…"

"…you had another such talk with your father, and in the heat of that argument, you spill everything out."

"Yes, and you know what he said?"

"*Hmm?*" I shook my head.

"*That is how family businesses are made, Veer. Look at how much your mummy and I have sacrificed for it.*" He smirked. I wish I knew what to say to him.

"You know, Adeeba, *didi* tells me she wanted to protect me when actually, she was saving herself. From this possibility."

"*Hmmm.*"

"She wanted to believe they didn't know about it. If they knew, they would fight for her. I swear, Adeeba, I wanted to believe that too."

"Veer…"

"But she didn't let me take a stand for her. I could do nothing, Adeeba!"

At that point, I wanted to tell him it was not his fault his parents were terrible. It was not his fault he could not fight for his sister. Sometimes, the people we love have demons to fight. Sometimes they trade fairness, or justice for never having to confront that fear. They shun our will to fight with them through that horror. They leave us with indelible marks of inadequacy, which bear demons who keep shouting that we failed them.

I wanted to tell him it was not his fault. I wanted to tell him I was proud of him, for he had not failed his sister or himself.

I wanted to tell him so many things, but like every other time, I choked. The sky was crimson from falling dusk, and our legs hanged down into the abyss. I clutched his hand tight.

"It will all be okay, Veer."

"*Hmmm.*"

10

Ruffles of her yellow dupatta slide down her arm as she stoops to take off her sandals; her breath is short from the uphill climb to the temple. Though a foreigner, the grace with which she carries herself in *salwar kurta* awes me. Sunlight laces through the lush green cedar trees surrounding the legendary Hidamba Temple. A pious, holy vibe wraps around the place as the temple bells ring in harmony with the astounding serenity.

"Why would you worship a demon?" She asks as she folds her leg to dust off her foot.

"Hidamba didn't remain a demon after she married a Pandava," I say.

"Adeeba, why would a Devata marry Hidamba?" She asks in a thick American accent.

"Hidamba lived in that cave," I say, pointing at the cave around which the temple was built, "with her arrogant brother Hidamb.

She had vowed she would only marry the man who defeated her brother. When the Pandavas came to this area, Hidamba fell in love with Bheem. At that, Hidamb got so angry he lashed out at him. In the fight, Bheem killed Hidamb. With their mother, Kunti's approval, Bheem married Hidamba.

After their marriage, Hidamba no longer remained a demon. The legend is as old as the Mahabharata."

"Maha...what?"

"Mahabharata," I chuckle. "The Hindu Epic."

"I love Indian stories, the myths, the folklore." A charismatic smile tears through her lips.

Every year, my city attracts tourists from around the globe. Foreign men treat me nothing like these men. They talk to me with respect. Even when they make moves, it is to seek consent. I feel safe in putting them down.

What I love the most about this foreign appeal of Manali, though, is that it brings to me women from different countries. It lets me spend time with them, take them around the city, get to know their stories. These women are the most beautiful I have ever met. Unlike the ones I have lived and grown with, they know how tailor-made they are for independence. They do not live by rules designed to hold them captive; they dictate how they should be treated. They own the elegance they have been created with, even the parts of them that stand against stereotypes. Most importantly, they do not weigh other women down.

So when they smile, they light me up with the freedom they encompass.

Just like this woman who sits beside me, exhausted from the trek, listening to stories I tell her about the place. Her amber eyes are twinning with her hair, which she has locked into a bun behind her head. Her cheeks gloss from the sweat that trickles down into her *kurta*. It must be leaving a ticklish impression between her breasts; she rubs her *kurta* against her cleavage every now and then. As she does, I see impressions on the cloth, of her saggy, round breasts bouncing freely beneath—she is not wearing a bra. Her lips are withered and rugged from days of travelling in the mountains. When she wets them with her tongue, though, they lustre. As her body rubs against mine, the muscles in my stomach clench. We laugh and fidget, exchanging life stories now.

She tells me she comes from Florida. Her father was a worker at the most enormous fishery corporation there. Her mother, a hippie who left her at his doorstep and fled. Even at that, the look on her face doesn't change. Her father is a gentleman she says; her stepmother is a bitch.

"My blood(y)-mother would rip her bitchy ass though," she chuckles at her pun, no hint of sadness in her tone. "Dad's retired now, lives with his eccentric wife, meets me on weekends."

"So you live alone?" I ask her.

"*Ah!* Nopes! I live with my wife," she replies nonchalantly, as if it were normal.

"Yes, Adeeba, I have a wife." She's so unapologetic I am falling for it already.

"Are you too…lesbian?"

"*Haha!* No. I am pansexual," she says.

"What is that?" I ask.

"*Ah*, okay! It means I get attracted to personalities, not any specific gender."

"*Umm…*"

I did not know something like that even existed. I only knew that I could like a man and be normal, or like a woman and hide it from the world. That is what my classmate had told me, long back when I was in school.

I had asked him why everyone called him *chakka*. "I didn't hide it well enough," he had said.

"Human biology is bizarre, darling," she says.

"It breaks stereotypes. Some men feel like they have a woman trapped inside. Some women choose to be called men. Some even both; some none. Some men like men, some women, women, Some like both, some none. That is why they call us rainbows."

"And your…wife? Is she also pansexual? Or lesbian?"

"She had an abusive marriage. Her bastard husband used to hit her. After she walked out of that marriage, she couldn't stand men around her. That's when she met me, and discovered the fantastic wife I could be. It's complicated; I don't know. All I know is that she loves me, and she's happy."

"It's scary. Not knowing who you are, then discovering it and making peace with it…"

"Of course, but at least you get to define who you want to be, and not live by definitions and choke yourself."

"No, you don't. You have to hide it."

"It's legal in the U.S. baby!" She winks.

"Oh, okay! *Umm…*"

"Chill darling! No one's gonna remember you for so long. Just fuck it, have tequila, and live the way you want."

A smile tears through her lips again. She pats at my thigh, and her touch runs an electric spark in my body. There is something to her energy; I am lost in her story. My mind is racing, stretching threads to their breaking points to join dots, to weave my story so that it looks similar to hers. Just so I could say *we are just the same.* A gentleman father—yes, *Baba* is a gentleman. A mother who did not care—I downgrade *Ammi*, only to feel guilty. A bitchy stepmother—I stop there. She is irresistible.

Will any man ever see her the way I just did? This woman, in front of me, is amazing. She is so perfect I do not want a man to relish her body and then break her heart. I want her to have someone who falls in love with her naked soul, and I know how rare are men who can do that.

We stand up, dust ourselves, and stroll around the temple, observing the flora and talking about it.

One of my favourite Greek stories talks of a village where barbarous men lived with their wives and children. Their lust for power was so intense they always picked battles with neighbouring clans. The wars lasted months, sometimes years, and exhausted many resources. The women and children starved without their breadwinners.

When one such battle prolonged, the women started working, taking care of their children and other women around them. They became sisters, and the realization started seeping in that they could fend for themselves. The happiness quotient of the village boomed like never before. Once they played with each other and found it amusing, they knew they did not need the men at all. Lesbianism started in that village as sisterhood.

When the men returned from battle, they could do nothing but yield to the women. That was the power of a united frontier of women. If only the women around me could understand that! If only *Ammi* had understood that! If only Sabeena had understood that!

We are in the rear of the temple premise, and the woman is obsessing over some wildflowers she spots. My eyes catch sight of that little boy from the other day, the one with Sabeena's eyes. As he runs through the gate, he screams:

"*Ammiiiiiiii!*"

Milky white complexion, dark brown hair, and big round eyes—Sabeena's eyes. His *Ammi* must be standing at the other side of the temple, where people gather to see the Hidamba Devi idol. He runs straight to her, trips over a stone and falls. His father appears from behind the temple. He picks him up and dusts off his scratched knee. I start walking towards the boy; the woman trails after me.

I am in my train of thoughts. The boy's mother stands in front of me, wearing a *burkha*. Her back faces me. As she turns, everything goes blank.

I jump behind the wall. I am shivering. My hands are cold, my forehead sweating. I do not know why I am so scared; I just am.

I steal a glance—she is joining hands along the side, in the way of *dua* in front of the idol. A lady then corrects her. As she joins her palms now, her son mimics her.

"Adeeba, what is wrong? What happened?" The tourist woman asks me, but I do not bother to reply. I am taking heavy, nervous breaths.

As the boy's mother walks past me, I hide my face. I am following her now, keeping a safe distance so she does not notice me. Will she, though? I do not know; it has been twelve years.

I follow them to their lodge. Sabeena has come to visit my city.

11

It was a winter afternoon when Sabeena had come running to me, again with that book of sonnets. I remember that day, that moment. The cold wind slipped in beneath the door, enough to blur the windows with dew.

A shivering Sabeena stood before me, or should I say a frozen, oscillating Sabeena? Cold weather did horrible things to her. I remember she was wearing three layers, the outermost sweater oversized and saggy, for it was mine. She had been sitting in the sun, reading from her favourite poet Maktub Ansari, until the wind had taken charge and chilled her to the bones.

I remember everything, for when your heart breaks, you do not forget it. It becomes a timestamp in your memory. You remember life before it, after it—some crystal clear memories, others disoriented and fuzzy. But the memory of life through it never blurs. So yes, I remember.

"*Appi*, explain this to me," she had said, handing me that book as I served hot porridge to her for lunch. That sonnet claimed to pass on Allah's *most important teaching*. It had caught my nerve before I had even finished reading it.

"*Appi*, what does it mean?" She had asked again.

"Sabeena, according to this poem, Allah says love should only exist between a man and a woman. *Matlab*, only to create new human beings love should happen. That is the divine purpose it is meant to serve. Anything happening without that purpose is just lust, and Allah forbids that."

"*Hmmm*. That is *toh* true only *na*?" She asked, rhetorically. Her nonchalance perturbed me.

"What! No. That is not true. Allah wouldn't say that!"

"Allah forbids that, *Appi*. *Ammi* also says that. Even *Maulvi Sahab* from the mosque says that."

"Sabeena, stop reading this idiot's poems first. He is the most narcissistic man ever. Tell me, do you think love exists only for this purpose?"

"No *Appi*. I can't say that. But if you love someone and you cannot have a family with them, what is the point in acting upon it?"

"Sabeena, that is so insensitive. So many couples do not have children, because one of them is infertile."

"That is different, *Appi*. I was talking about only a man and a woman thing."

"What is wrong with that?"

"The purpose of love is missing."

"Sabeena, love is not for any purpose." I almost screamed. "You do not choose who you get attracted to. It is how our bodies have been made. You cannot change it."

"No, *Appi*, it is a state of mind. A true muslim would never go against Allah's commandments."

"Sabeena, attraction is physical. The mind is not involved. Think of our bodies as machines that Allah makes. Don't some machines from any factory turn out to be defective? Although, that is a very wrong word. I should say…different."

"No, *Appi*. Allah is perfect. He does not make mistakes."

At that point, I stopped. I knew she would not understand. She was blind, like *Ammi*, to an entire spectrum that existed between the binary the world had set. I swallowed a lump; the secret of my reality, the part of me I could not change, was breaking loose on me. Allah had denied me my sister.

What did Sabeena know about love? What could she know about love? My little sister was just thirteen, reading a poet who wrote of love like a blind man describes a rainbow—something beautiful made of colours, no existence of itself, a divine ornament to adorn a weeping sky. Why should a narcissistic man like him mould my sister's tangible, adolescent thoughts into shapes that would eat up her individuality? Was he the only one to a fault? Were *Ammi* and Maulvi Sahab not equally responsible? Why should they implant incorrigible opinions in her about feelings she had not even experienced yet? Or had she—if you would pass that little thing she had for the boy in her class as love.

Yes, Sabeena had felt something for someone. Her best friend or I should say her only friend, Bani, had told me. He was Bani's friend, or rather her boyfriend's friend. Our school was in Mahabaleshwar, and it often felt like the local town kids had been raised in a parallel world. They were open to falling in love, even to falling out of it. Then falling in love again, with someone else. They called it infatuation.

Bani and that boy were those kids. Sabeena was not.

They would sit together every recess, and eat from each other's lunches. Sabeena seldom took a lunch box to school. Having no lunch was better than having something no one wanted to share. She sat at an arm's length from him, his tiffin between them. She loved the *misal poha* he brought. That is all Sabeena had ever told me about him, every time I had asked her.

"Say *na*, Subbu, you love him *na*? You love him *na*?" I would tease her, poke her with a finger in the stomach.

"*Nahi Appi*, there is nothing like that. You're just cooking stories to get me beaten by *Ammi*," she would say, withdrawing from me, her lips struggling not to break into a smile.

Sabeena was in love, the kind of love *she* had defined for herself. I knew it, for she smiled vacantly all day, and froze in front of him the way you do when you meet your *shauhar* for the first time. Bani would often disappear with her boyfriend in the middle of their lunch, leaving the two by themselves. They would finish their lunch and stroll in the campus fields. Sometimes they ate *samosas*, which he paid for always.

How long, though, before the trance that love is in the beginning started to fade? How long before the butterflies in her stomach settled down? Love always casts an enchanting spell around you. It makes you go to great lengths after it. Sabeena had too—she had ignored that the boy was not Muslim. When the spell breaks, though, it uncovers to you the little ugly nuances of falling in love with a person who is not the same as you thought them to be. It then tests you with the weight of those realizations. You see, all fancies resemble love, but love has its ways of sorting them out.

Sabeena could not bear the longing; she was barely a teenager after all. She did not know if he felt the same for her, if he loved her, let alone if he would marry her. And what good was love if it did not end in marriage? Plus, it is only maidenly of little girls to shy away from love. So she decided to wait.

She withdrew from that group of friends. She wanted him to come after her, but it was not happening. Her absence was not hurting him. She was pretending she did not bother either. Every night in her bed, though, she wept as she failed to crumple a wish to which, now, she would dare not latch any hope.

One day she saw him sharing his *missal poha* with a girl much more beautiful than her. His eyes twinkled just the way hers did at him. My little girl's heart broke.

That night, for the first time, she talked to me about it. She held me tight across my belly, just like she would when she was little. She told me he did not love her, that she would only hurt herself if she continued. She asked me to pinch her hard whenever she thought of him. When Bani asked her about it, she fought with her so hard that she had almost lost her only friend.

Sabeena had resolved to dump the mess of her feelings, and my sister was good at achieving what she determined.

Why would Allah do this to us, though? If Allah was the master of the universe, why should his decrees be rules and not laws? If he had created everything— Sabeena, me, *Ammi,* Bhoomi, men, the world, so on, why did he allow the things he forbade to exist? If Allah did not want his women to love men outside the religion, why would he let Sabeena feel what she did? If he did not want me to love a woman, why would he engineer me to have those feelings? If Allah resided inside all of us, if he resided inside me, why would he live alongside feelings that were blasphemous to him? Why should I lose my sister, my mother, because I loved a woman? Why did Allah let me open my heart to love and then expect me to stitch it close again in his name?

I felt lonely, as if I were on a train, in some foreign country—perspiring bodies rubbing against each other, pushing, moving, adjusting, budging for personal space. My eyes roved outside the window for Sabeena, who was running towards the gate to get on board.

The gates started closing. She sprinted, waving out to me to stop, but I could not. She was panting now, sobbing as well; the train had picked up pace. I was budging, screaming, shouting, crying, but my desperate attempts to shake the world were not causing as much as ripples even. They talked to each other, about politics, or sports, or economics, music, or maybe porn, in a language I did not know. They could not hear me, see me, touch me. The train had left the platform to enter a tunnel. Sabeena had been shut out. I did not know where it was going.

There was only one hand I could hold now; a hand I could not ever leave. When I had hugged Bhoomi that evening, she did not know why the hug was so tight. She was cooking chapattis for dinner. In her usual nonchalance, she had said,

"*Aa gayi, rona rone? Kya hua ab?*" (You've come again, to cry here? What happened now?)

"Loose motion," I said. Her forehead wrinkled and her nostrils inflated till her nose looked like a potato.

"Cheeeeee!" She whined, slapping me on the arm. We chuckled.

Bhoomi fumbled haphazardly between the kitchen boxes for carom seeds. She was a kitchen perfectionist; so her dough could not do without that characteristic *azwain* flavour. She was half an inch away from finding it, and equidistant from total panic. As I stood beside her, I could not help myself not drool in her admiration. She was beautiful, perfect. Or was she? I did not know. All I knew was that something had changed in the way I looked at her.

Why is the moon so important to humans, to literature and romance? When the sun is the source of life, when it is the stars which have all the light, when it is the space that accommodates the earth, why do the poets compare their lovers to the moon? It is because the moon has craters. It is not all powerful or self-fulfilling like the stars. It is needy, imperfect yet beautiful, and therefore approachable. It is the most faithful companion. It shows up every night without fail, for the poets to muse and the travellers to get lost. The sun can be scorching and blinding, but the moon stands in the way. It takes all the heat and shines through it, passing on only enough to soothe us. So in the nights when it is not there, everything is dark and hopeless.

Bhoomi had become my moon.

"Bhoomi…" I said.

"Hmm?"

"I love you…" I stuttered. "I love you Bhoomi. I will do anything for you."

At that she turned. Her stare was uneasy, as if something fuzzy and scratchy crawled beneath my skin.

"*Chal phir*," she said, breaking the silence. "Knead this into your finest dough for me," she completed, sliding forward her vessel full of flour towards me, breaking into laughter.

"Yeah, except that, of course," I said, and laughed with her.

12

My head is crammed with thoughts about that temple visit as I serve *puris* to *Baba* and Veer. My horrid past is seeping up through years of burial.

When Sabeena was just five-six years old, she would get all wimpy at the thought of me marrying a man and leaving her to live with *Ammi*. So whenever she was up to some mischief, which mostly comprised fighting with boys, that was my favourite thing to say. She would start crying—I would get to hug her. Then she punched me in the stomach with her little fist and separated.

"I will come along with you, *aapan thamba ani paha*," she grunted.

"But I will have my own children then. Who will take care of you?"

"I will beat your children," she would say, with ballooned cheeks which I kissed to burst. "*Huh! Appi,* you're so bad." She would wipe the moist imprint on her cheek.

My little Sabeena is a mother now. She is a married woman, with a *shauhar*, a son so full of life just like her, and a home to make. She is happy.

For the past twelve years, I have yearned for her every day. Every day I have imagined a parallel universe, where we did not separate but grew together. In those daydreams, Sabeena plans my wedding. Even before I murmur the first *'Qubool hai'*, she will already have had a private conversation with my *shauhar*, warning him against any tear I should shed after marriage. She will be all robust and in charge of everything during the *nikaah*. But as soon as I step on the threshold, she will become her wimpy little self again. She will press her face in my chest and wail, her tears so infectious everyone will start sobbing. I am scared she will love my children more than hers.

Yet when I saw her yesterday, I froze. It is funny how convenient reveries can be. What are they, if not self-woven stories? People behave according to me; life moves according to me. Yesterday does not have to be consistent with today or tomorrow. The episodes can always complement my mood. Most importantly, if I fuck up somewhere, I just have to rethink that scene.

Reality, on the other hand, is so uncomfortable. I have longed for my sister for years, but now that she is so close, I want to run away. How will I face her, when all I have given her is abandonment and a limping leg?

I wanted to disappear until these thoughts settled, but Veer would not let that happen. Sometimes his paranoia of losing me is too much to take. The previous night he was upset at not having seen my paintings, and I slept while texting.

Veer: Why can't you just let me in?

Veer: Why do I always have to make such strong efforts just to be in your life?

Veer: I tell you everything, but you hardly do.

Veer: We have been together for almost a year.

Veer: Why can't I meet your family?

Obviously, he deleted all of that, but it did not disappear from my notifications.

Veer: Was sending it to an associate.

Adeeba: Chutiya samjhe ho na?

Veer: Sorry :(

Adeeba: Tomorrow at 2. My place. Baba doesn't like late people.

Veer: I love you. :))))))))))))

It is four in the evening; Bhoomi is asleep. *Baba* and Veer's political views align so much he does not want to leave for his evening walk. Veer is on seventh heaven for having made his dream first impression. He smiles like you do when your teacher praises you in a parent-teacher's meet, except he is not ten. As I look at them with a blurred gaze, I must be smiling. I am not pissed with Veer. I am just not in the right frame of mind. And he is not entirely wrong. I do keep him at arm's length, not far but never close enough.

"*Beta ji,*" *Baba* says to Veer, with a morsel still in his mouth, "I must go to the temple now, or I shall miss the *aarti.*"

"*Ji* uncle, okay," Veer replies in a mellow, honorary tone. *Baba* gestures me to come with him as he heads towards the sink.

"He is a nice man. Serve him your *lassi*, but make sure he leaves soon after. You girls shall be alone." My *lassi* has always been *Baba's* favourite thing to flaunt.

"*Hmm, Baba.* I'll take care."

"Good."

Baba picks his walking stick and leaves. And no sooner has the door slammed than Veer jumps across the sofa in excitement.

"Your father loves me now," he says with a playful sniff.

"*Ah-ha!* He only liked your political banter," I smirk.

"No way! There was more than just that."

"...and perhaps your tuxedo, *huh?*" I raise a brow, and all his excitement blurs into a blush.

"It was my first time. I wanted it to be perfect."

"You're cute," I chuckle.

"Yeah, now stop."

He gets out of his coat and steps forth to hug me. I swear I need it, but my head is jammed.

"What's wrong, Adeeba?" I have not hugged back.

"*Ah!* Nothing."

"Look, I shouldn't have deleted those messages."

"I read them. So chuck it."

"Adeeba I am sorry. I was just impulsive, you know me."

"It's fine."

"No, it's not. I do that all the time. I feel terrible."

"Veer! Chill. I mean it. It's fine."

"If you say so!" We sit on the sofa, and keep sitting until I break the silence.

"So…the art gallery."

"Yes, yes, where is it?"

"Come."

"Wait, have I earned it now?" He says. I grin.

"Yes, you have." He walks after me.

A musty odour charges at us as I thrust the door open. I have not opened the room in a month; all surfaces lie blanketed in dust. As Veer unveils one of my landscapes, dust gets into his nose. The room echoes with his sneeze.

"It's amazing, *yaar*," he says, rubbing his nose.

"Thank you, Veer."

One by one, we stroll through my paintings. For each of my landscapes, I tell him a backstory—the inspiration behind it, how many days it took to paint, how much time for the oil to dry, about the mistakes, how I fixed them, everything. He listens to me with all the intent, though I know he is not understanding a thing. He does that always. It takes me little to tell if Veer is truly interested in something I say—whenever he is not, he overcompensates.

We have now reached the five portraits—*Baba*, Bhoomi, Veer, Sabeena and *Ammi,* in order. I am not sure if we should go further, but Veer will not stop. He uncovers *Baba's* portrait.

"Oh my god! This is so cool!"

"Thanks!" He was waiting for the backstory now; I had nothing to say.

"What happened? You painted *Baba's* portrait. That's so awesome. Tell me about it."

"There's nothing to know." I steal my gaze; he notices that.

"Adeeba, what is it? Are you pissed with me?"

"No!" He gives me a steady glare. "What?" I ask.

"Doesn't look like it."

"Like what? *Yaar*, Veer!"

"Anyway, next painting!" He sighs. I uncover Bhoomi's portrait.

"*Ah!* Another family member." He says.

"I painted this when I had had a fight with her. She didn't talk to me for two months straight. This was my sorry gift to her." Yes, I make up this backstory; I do not have the headspace for more retorts.

"Adeeba, can I ask you something?"

Yaar, nai. Abhi nai, I want to shout. But all I say is, "Yes, *pucho*?"

"*Baba* said he was going to a *temple*, right?"

"*Hmm*?" I nod. I know where he is going.

"And Bhoomi also seems…*uh*…Hindu name. Then how come you are Muslim? And who is Bhoomi to you?"

I swallow a lump; I have no answer. What should I tell him—that *Baba* adopted two girls who had been thrown out of their village, that my only fault was trying to save Bhoomi? And if I tell him this much, will it stop there?

No. He will know I am a lesbian. All my feelings will become a lie to him then.

"I don't…I don't want to discuss this right now."

"Adeeba! I can't live with so many questions. Answer me."

"Veer please!"

"Why always? Why do you dodge my questions?"

"Not right now, please. Pleaseee!" I whimper.

"Okay. Okhaayyyy!" He let out heavy breaths to compose himself. "When? Tell me when."

"I…I don't know…what to say."

"Of course! Don't say anything. Don't. I'll understand. I'll have to understand."

"Veer…no…please…" I say, in a shrill, weightless voice. I hold his hand but he jerks it away.

"I don't understand where I fail. Why do I always get pushed away? I just…want to feel…I don't know, important? Because I told you things I had never told anyone. But you…you wouldn't trust me. Why, am I not…*huh*!"

"Veer, don't say that, please. You know you're important. Very important."

"So important that you cannot tell me anything about yourself?" His eyes water.

"I don't know how you will react to it." *Arghh!* Pathetic choice of words!

"Wow! That is what you think of me." He says, raising his brows.

"No…no no no no! Veer, I…shit…I didn't mean that. I just don't know what to say."

"And I don't know if I should believe you anymore—believe that I am important, that you will ever let me into your life, not keep me distant from everything. Don't try to save me. Stop hiding behind this lie."

I have never seen him this cold. I am weeping, but he does not even look at me. Unlike always, he does not tell me it is okay, that he understands. And why should he? To what length should he understand me? I have always been free to act moody, get angry, not make any first moves. He cannot always come after me. Even when he is angry, his anger is so flimsy it does not stand as much as a tender tone of my voice. It feels like we have switched places. I feel everything I have made him feel, and I do not know how to deal with it.

"I love you, Veer," My words fritter into sobs.

He snuffs, rolling his eyes at me. "I don't even know who you are."

At that, I break. I should not have let this happen. What other fate could a relationship built on unkempt secrets have? I know he will beat himself up over this. He will let himself believe he lacked somewhere. If only he could hate me after this! I would get my atonement. But he will not. I know, for when I start crying, the stern look on his face melts. My mind is racing. I want to make up to him. I jerk the cloth that covered his portrait.

"All the portraits here are people who are my family. I have kept secrets from you; I am guilty of that. But Veer, I love you…I love you…I love you."

My wails halt for deep breaths, as I wait for him to say something. But he stands frozen; his empty glance shot at me. His fingers vibrate, his lips flutter, but his legs are grounded.

"I…I am…adopted. *Baba* is not…*mere asli Abbu nahi hain wo.* I will tell you everything. E-v-e-r-y-t-h-i-n-g! I will answer all your questions. But don't be angry, please. I can't take it."

A bulb of tear draws into a stream as it trickles down his cheek. As his feet move towards me, my heart thuds against my chest. And before I realize, his lips stick to mine. "I don't care, Adeeba. I…love you," his breath storms at my philtrum.

I open my mouth and let his tongue explore. His fingers claw at my scalp. As he sucks on my upper lip, his cologne mixes with sweat and bursts inside my nostrils. His moustache pricks my skin; the pain escalates my heartbeat. And just when I am all into the kiss, he clutches my hair and pulls me away. As he does so, his eyes meet mine—goosebumps on my arms. I am not going to stop him; not today. He deserves that I kiss him, though it is platonic on my part.

He grabs me tight around my waist and lifts me with a jerk. As he presses me against the wall, the dust on it laces my hair. My face gets plugged into his neck. I want to kiss it, lick it, bite upon it.

Our breaths have intensified, our eyes closed. His hand slides down my back, from hair to the buttocks.

As he squeezes them, it seems a current runs down my spine. Then his lips scramble down to my neck. He kisses it before he bites—everything I have read about love-bites is true. His hands then slither up to my chest; his lips venture for a kiss again. He unbuttons my *kurti* and slides his hand inside. Why am I not resisting? Something strange is happening to me. As his coarse, manly fingers skid over my tender breasts, the friction of it fills me with ecstasy. My nipples are hard now. As his lips separate from mine, I let out heavy breaths.

His tongue licks between my breasts now; my fingers caress his hair. My body is ablaze; I moan. What is happening? My body is betraying me. How can I…why am I not stopping him? Do I even want to stop? Why is my body tampering with everything I believe myself to be? It is not right, but why does it not feel wrong?

He grabs my hand and puts it between his legs, where his slim fit pants cover an erection. I catch myself wanting to unzip him and take his penis in my hands. As he rubs upon my *salwar*, the wet patch of cloth makes it uneasy between my legs.

"Veer, stop…" I manage to let out, but he shuts me up with a kiss. My mind and body have segregated. My body has resigned to the sheer pleasure of being touched by him. My mind cannot fathom why.

"Veer please stop!"

"*Ummmm*…Adeeba …" He continues to kiss me all over.

My existential crisis has resurfaced now. My head is bursting. Who am I? Am I not a lesbian woman who lives with her mentally impaired lesbian lover? If that is true, why is my body rejoicing the touch of a man? If not true, why have I taken so much trouble? Why did I give up my family to save Bhoomi from a nasty ritual? Why did I let Sabeena sacrifice her leg to save me from being killed for that? Do I not love Bhoomi? Do I not love Veer? How differently?

Nothing is pleasant anymore. His kisses burn my skin. That intimacy smothers me. It all feels like an act of treachery I have committed against Bhoomi.

"Veer stop! Please." I say. He tries kissing my lips again. I turn my face away, so he drops down to my neck.

"Veer stop!" I repeat, my voice a little stern this time.

"You want it too Adeeba. You're wet," he says, and resumes kissing my shoulders, then my arms. But it is too much to take now. In the fit of perplexed thoughts, I push him so hard he gets thrown on the floor.

"What the fuck!" He shouts.

"I am a lesbian," I scream back, and everything freezes.

"I didn't know you would go to this length to find an excuse."

Tears do not stop dripping from my eyes. He gets up, buttons himself and storms out of the room, out of the house. I run after him, helplessly crying, shouting out to him to stop, but he does not.

As he slams the door behind him, my legs give way. I fall on the sofa beside me, weeping as if there is no life beyond this moment.

"What happened, *didi*?" I hear from behind. Bhoomi has woken up.

"Nothing." I say.

13

Dear Veer,

I am writing to you because tere samne mujhse kuch nahi bola jayega.

Main darr gayi thi. If you got to know everything, you would leave me. Not because you wouldn't be able to take it, but because only that shall be fair. I should not have fallen in love with you. I should not have let you love me. I should not have...but I did.

To answer your questions, Baba mere asli Abbu nahi hain. He adopted Bhoomi and me when we were thrown out of our village. And yes, I am a lesbian, or at least so I have believed for thirteen years of my life. Ever since I kissed Bhoomi. Now you know who she is. There is so much I need to tell you, and I don't know how to tie everything together.

I was born in Rohila, a village near Mahabaleshwar. I lived there with my Ammi and little sister Sabeena. My Abbu had passed away when I was eight. Since Ammi had to take up some work...

I have not heard from Veer ever since that episode. He has deactivated his WhatsApp, and he will not take my calls. Writing emails is the only option left. So I sit in the café where his sister plays in the evenings, documenting my life story in PDFs, on a laptop Veer only gifted me. No, I am not going to talk to her.

I have told *Baba* I would be late—the tourists are flocking to Manali as Diwali is at hand. It is 7:30 in the evening, but I do not want to go home. I do not know where I want to go. It feels like everything that belonged to me does not anymore. I feel like a stranger in my own body. My *Baba*, Bhoomi, my city and even my past, everything belonged to the Adeeba I no longer am.

I am going to tell him everything; I start with my family. I talk about *Ammi,* her afternoon stories and her life struggle, then about Sabeena. After that, I tell him about Bhoomi, how I met her, our school stories, about our families, and finally about that kiss. At this point, I am scared—will he continue reading?

Veer's sister is at the piano now—stark silence in the cafe. Beside her, there is a bowl wherein customers can drop song requests. The placard behind her reads *NO TIPS*. On most tables, people are scribbling on tissue papers now. And even before she has as much as pressed the first key, her jar is half full.

I shift my focus back to my screen. I am to tell him what changed all our lives. My fingers start shivering. It is tough to form sentences now.

...but one day, everything changed. We were seventeen then. Bhoomi's parents had started looking for grooms. That quest had begun at my home as well. We used to sit in the evenings in sheer silence. We didn't want to part from each other, but what choice did we have?

I don't know how or when, but the villagers learned that Bhoomi had not undergone Khatna. The entire village erupted at Bhoomi's parents. Such rage I had never seen before...

Rohila had a ritual, as nasty as it could be. The men of the village talked very highly of that ancient inhumane practice. The women nodded after them, for that was the most they could say. But Khatna was the reality of every girl in Rohila, be it *Ammi*, Sabeena, Bhoomi's mother or any other woman. Yes, me as well.

They cut off the clitoral hood and the labia. They almost sealed the vagina, so she could not have sex. They only left a small hole for them to urinate and bleed. The stitches would open in the night of her marriage when her husband penetrated her.

In Rohila, this ceremony happened as soon as girls turned six. So their parents had to save for this, too, alongside dowry. Traditional midwives performed it— no anesthesia, unhygienic conditions. No disinfected scissors or knives, but broken pieces of glass. They tied her legs apart for weeks to let the wound heal. I have known many women who died of the septic infections it caused.

Still, the men chanted in the name of the ritual. Religious purity they called it. The women nodded after them.

…yes, Veer. It has happened to me too. But unlike Ammi, Bhoomi's parents didn't place that ritual above their daughter. When she was born, Bhoomi's parents went to her nani's village. They didn't return until Bhoomi was nine. When they did, everyone had forgotten about it…

The villagers felt bluffed. They kept shouting outside Bhoomi's house. They even pelted stones and broke all their windows. Some acid balls as well. The nasty mob had men of all ages—grandfathers, fathers, boisterous young men, boys, and even kids. Their weapons of choice comprised cricket bats, wickets, tube lights, leather belts and whatnot. The women in veils formed clusters outside their houses to badmouth Bhoomi's parents.

I was inside the house with a shivering Bhoomi. Beside us sat Bhoomi's mother, weeping her *dupatta* to a pulp. Just then, Sabeena came running, saying *Ammi* had sent for me. I wanted to stay with Bhoomi, but I knew *Ammi* would beat Sabeena up if I did not go. The next day, there were decoration arrangements outside her house. Her mother told me they were having the ceremony two days later.

Bhoomi was beyond petrified. She would not stop crying, and there was nothing I could say that could calm her. She had seen girls being infibulated. If I told her it was any less painful than it looked, I would be lying.

…I could not let her be a victim to something so brutal. So I decided we would elope. I had no plan. I didn't know where we would go. But if that was the only way to save Bhoomi, I would do it.

Of course, she didn't take me seriously. Neither did my sister when she saw me packing my clothes. I made Sabeena swear she wouldn't tell Ammi about it, and she complied.

The following morning, I slithered out of my house at three. I had made Bhoomi swear she would meet me at the back of her house, so there she was. I didn't say or hear anything from her. I just held her hand and ran…

It was not morning yet; the village was asleep. But whenever we spotted anyone, we hid behind carts, heaps of hay and whatnot. But for a goddamn washerwoman, we would have escaped. But she saw us, and did not stop screaming until she had woken everyone up. Of course, she knew.

…You should have seen the rage. Bhoomi and I could think of nothing else. If we stopped, they would kill me. Bhoomi would still have to go through that.

So we ran, and they ran after us, the men with lathis and grass blades, the women with thappis. They hit me with a lathi on my buttock. It was so hard I fell. Bhoomi received a similar blow… at the back of her head. She fell against her face. Her hair was laced in blood; she had fainted.

That didn't kill the mob's rage, though. They were all angry men; they looked deadly. One of them, who stood at my feet, swung his lathi through a reflex angle's arc. It was going to break my leg…but it didn't. Someone jumped on me, and it hit them instead. I knew the scream, though. It was Sabeena…

Ammi took Sabeena in her arms and started crying. The women had reached by then. The local *Vaidya* advised them to rush Bhoomi and Sabeena to the nearest hospital. I dropped from everyone's attention except *Ammi's*. When no one was watching, she said to me I was dead to her.

…Enter Baba. When the local inspector came to interview Sabeena and Bhoomi, Baba was the constable accompanying him. The villagers made some shitty excuse, but Baba wouldn't buy that. He wanted to know the true story, and of all people, he was lucky to pick me…

As I lift my gaze from the laptop, a boy drops a chit in the jar. I know who he is—Sabeena's son, my nephew. He runs back to a table where a woman sits in *burkha*, with a man I know is her husband. I should walk up to her, meet her, hug her, but I have resigned to my fears. I look into my screen again.

…Our reality shook baba. He had yearned for a child all his life. He couldn't believe people let their children go through something like that. So he urged the inspector to dig deeper into the investigation. And given Baba's reputation, he complied.

Back in Rohila, the impending outrage was too much to contain. They wanted to get done with the ritual. Had Baba not accompanied us, I don't know what they would have done to me. When Baba threatened them with law, they turned to the Gram

Panchayat. But even the Panches didn't know that they could not make the ritual happen...

So they decreed upon us a punishment. They sentenced that Bhoomi and I be excommunicated from Rohila. Our families could not come with us; they would have to continue living in Rohila.

As we were walked out of the village, the villagers stayed inside their houses—we were a disgrace. At Bhoomi's door, her parents stood weeping. At my door, there was only Sabeena, standing on her *baisakhi*, biting her lip so *Ammi* did not hear her sobs from inside the house. Bhoomi could not make new memories, so she forgot. But I remember that pain, every bit of it. Perhaps it is that separation. Though my sister is sitting right in front of me, we are still twelve years away. And I do not know how to walk that distance.

...Bhoomi could not make new memories anymore. That part of her brain was dead. Sabeena would limp for the rest of her life. And I was the reason.

After we left Rohila, Baba adopted us. He has been the best father ever. We moved to Manali because he wanted to live in the mountains. This became my life—caring for Baba, for Bhoomi. This remained my life, for twelve years. Then one day I met you.

With you, I don't know, I didn't hate myself. You loved me, cared for me, pampered me, and I fell for it. I knew all along that I was a lesbian, but I couldn't hold myself. I thought it was pure, platonic love. I hated myself for being selfish to you...until I realized that I was not.

When you kissed me, I don't know what happened to me. It felt like I liked that, wanted that. How could that be? I still don't know. I don't even know who I am anymore...

Sabeena turns and sees me. Her brows raise as she bites her nail. Maybe it is her long lost sister, but how can she be sure? As I make eye contact with her, she jerks her head away. But her gaze returns to me when I look into my laptop. Everything repeats when I look up. The nervous energy because of her presence is oozing out of me. It is almost like I am playing with her now.

...Tell me, Veer. How could I tell you all this? How does one know all this and not hate me? Anyway, I have told you everything. Life is blurry, hazy, shaky right now. But I love you. I know this for sure. I never wanted to hurt you.

Meet me, please. For once, even if you'll never meet me again.

Apologies,
Adeeba Sheikh.

Sabeena is walking towards me. My hands shiver. My legs freeze, and I cannot make eye contact with her anymore.

"*Appi*...Adeeba *Appi*? Ya Allah!" She exclaims. She stoops down and hugs me. My body flushes out loads of sweat, and tears ooze out of my eyes.

"Where were you *Appi*?" She asks, now nervous that I might be someone else. I'm still frozen.

Just when she is about to withdraw, I tighten my arms around her. I break down. The whole café is watching us now.

"Sabeena…I…I missed you. I…I am…sorry."

14

"*Appi*, you want tea?" Sabeena asks me from the table where the electric kettle is kept.

"No, Sabeena. I am good," I say, as I shield myself against her son's pillow whacks. His name is Sohrab, and I am his best friend now. It is a fine morning, and we are sitting in the lodge where they are staying. Her husband is out to visit a relative he has in the city.

She comes with her cup and sits by my side.

"*Appi,* I'm so happy we came for our holiday to Manali. *Alhamdulillah!* How could I ever have found you otherwise?" She says. My eyes fill with tears.

"I am sorry...Sabeena...I..."

"*Shhhhh!* Don't start with that now." She shuts me up.

Sabeena starts telling me about her family. She lives in Mahabaleshwar with Sohrab, her husband, and her typical mother-in-law—dilutes her spaghetti, instigates her son, does not give her a say in the house's finances.

But her husband supports her. He takes care of her.

"What else does one need, *hai na*?" She asks me. I am happy for her.

"What about *Ammi*, Sabeena? Where is she? How is she?"

"*Ammi* is no more, *Appi*." Her face shrinks.

"What? How…when?"

"After you left, *Ammi* became miserable, as if her backbone was broken. The villagers weren't easy on her either. She begged of contractors for work to keep herself busy.

'I am saving for your *nikaah*,' she would say. And rightly so, because the moment I turned sixteen, she became hyper-bent on getting me married. She married me off within a year.

After that, she lost her will to live, it seemed. She gave up working. She wouldn't eat for days. I would beg her to eat, but what could I achieve through phone calls? She seldom listened to me. All she did was miss you. 'Where must she be? How would my Adeeba be keeping herself? Bring me my daughter. I want to see her before *Allah* calls me.'

One day, I received a letter. She was no more."

I cannot contain myself. I hug her tight and burst into tears.

"I thought…she…*Ammi* hated me…"

"No, *Appi*. How could she hate you? She was your mother. She didn't like what you did, but she could never hate you," she says, caressing my hair.

I remember *Ammi's* words again. *In hearts of the people we love, we see reflections of ourselves.* All this while, they have been true.

When you look into a mirror, you see a reflection of yourself. You believe it to be your true representation. If you look good, you feel confident. If not, you rush to your closet, find a different outfit and do your hair all over. In the same way, when you love someone, you are vulnerable to them. The way you feel around them influences what you think of yourself. How they treat you can become your metric for how you should be treated. What they give you, you think you deserve.

When Sabeena and I were young, I felt guilty when I looked at her. She did not make me feel so; I had fixed notions against her. I thought she was not beautiful; I pitied her because I believed the world would not treat her well. I thought it would make her vengeful of me.

I thought *Ammi* hated me because I believed I deserved it. I had chosen Bhoomi over her, over Sabeena. I had chosen something against her faith in Allah. But had I stayed put and let Bhoomi suffer, I would have felt no different.

For the same reason, when I looked at *Baba*, I saw a good daughter in myself. So yes, they were mirrors, clean and unbiased mirrors. When I looked at them, I saw my own feelings reflected. What happens, though, when you look into broken or stained mirrors? What happens when you love people who are scarred?

You see the stains on your own reflection. You start believing that the scars are on you, that you are the dirty one. It haunts me to think what Sabeena must have seen. I had always wanted to protect her from people who made her conscious of her scar, never realizing that I believed it marred her beauty. I had always feared she would get vengeful of me, never realizing that I thought I was prettier than her.

And Veer. He was just as broken as I was. He did not know why he feared being distant or losing me. He did not know, but he sought his worth in solving problems for me, or his *didi*. Every day he fought his demons to believe he was just as worthy of love without that.

When he had discovered his sister's misery, he wanted to fight his parents for her. He wanted to get her justice, but she did not let him. He was carrying that scar, and his inexpressive girlfriend only made it worse for him. So he over-loved. So he spent every ounce of himself trying to prove his love to me, which made me feel guiltier about myself.

Ammi used to tell a story about a mighty demon who never returned to the villages he had ravaged once. The catch was that if someone called out his name, he would lose all his diabolical powers. The funny thing is that our scars are just like that demon—they lose their power when we become conscious of them.

It is not our fault if we have had a horrid past, but it is our responsibility to recognize our wounded parts and heal them. We can either be broken and bleeding, or heal ourselves and be tougher than ever.

I want to be the latter.

15

"What are they doing, *Appi?*"

"They are flying paper lanterns."

"*Arre!*" Sabeena chuckled. "That I know, but why?"

The sun has set; it is evening now. I have brought Sabeena and Sohrab to a spot in the city which I thought they would like. It is open land which ends in abyss.

"It's *Chhoti Diwali* today. Every year they come here to fly paper lanterns and make wishes. It's a custom of the place," I say. She nods.

"Come, let's buy a lantern, Sabeena" I say, pointing at a stall.

"*Unka parv hai Appi, hum thode hi manayengey,*" She says, almost instinctively.

"Why not?" I ask.

"*Umm…achha theek hai*," she says. We head towards the stall.

Sohrab is pressing against my leg as he walks, though, as if he were scared. At the stall, too, he is jerking his leg as though he were warding something off.

"What happened, *beta*?" I ask him.

"*Thaala (Khaala),* flies," he says, in his stammering voice. It is then I realize they are so many. Fireflies!

They are everywhere.

"They are harmless, Sohrab," I say, picking him up. As his butt rests on my arm, I kiss his cheek.

"But why are they burning."

"They are not burning, *beta*. They are just glowing."

"Yes, but why, *Thaala?*"

"Because they cannot buy light bulbs, so Allah gave them their own light."

"*Oh*…okay," he muttered.

As we walk towards the festivity, Sabeena unwraps the lantern and inflates it. She adjusts the candle; it takes a flying shape. It is November now, and it has rained in the afternoon. The air is cold by both means. The wet dust makes patterns on the grassless patches of the ground.

As I look up, I get lost in the serenity of the sky. There is me, Sabeena, Sohrab, and all the people around. Then there is a dying crescent of the moon above. And in between, I see an army of yellow lamps, on a mission to fetch the stars their king must have promised his queen.

People wear their finest clothes, click pictures to capture moments from their holiday to Manali. Some young couples stand at the barricade, as near as they can get to the abyss. Scattered all over, the fireflies try their best to mimic the stars in the sky. In fact, Sohrab is not the only kid there who is scared of them.

"*Thaala*, why don't we collect some of them in a bottle? We can use that as a light bulb," he asks me.

"Many people do that, but it is wrong, *beta*."

"But why?"

"Because just like you, that poor insect must be having his *Ammi* around somewhere," I play along.

"Then we will put her also in the bottle, *na*?"

"How will you know which one she is?"

"*Alle, haan!*"

I kiss his cheek again. Many years ago, I lost my family. Today, I have two. I close my eyes and remember Allah, not to ask for anything, but to thank him. And as I do so, my phone buzzes.

Veer: I am returning to Manali in six days. I'll meet you then.

I can only ever not smile.

As Sabeena lights up the lantern, Sohrab jumps from my lap, all excited about flying it.

"I'll fly it, *Ammi*. I'll fly it." He starts whining. She gives it to him but does not let her fingers off it until the air inside has heated and the lantern holds shape.

As she leaves it, it tends to go up. Sohrab lets his hand rise along with it. He starts running forward. When his hand is almost vertical, he takes a leap.

"*Yayyy!*" He exclaims as he releases his fingers.

The lantern flies.

ACKNOWLEDGEMENTS

Before I say thanks, I would like to mention that Rohila is a fictitious place. So is Kainat. The birth curse is also fictitious, but I wish I could say the same about infibulation. It is still in practice in some parts of the world, and some population in India practises it too. Although, in the story, I have taken the artistic liberty to call it *Khatna*, and any resemblance to a real place, person, thing or practice is purely coincidental.

Now if you have read it this far, thank you. Thank you for reading my book, and giving me the most important thing you could—your time.

I believe I have been blessed to feel too much and observe very closely. And my stories are a reflection of that. Although my characters are fictitious, what they feel is real. They draw heavily from my life, and the lives of people around me. So these people I mention here have been much more a part of my journey than I can ever tangibly show.

To my family—thank you for letting me walk this *road not taken*. Guys, no one in my family has ever written a book, let alone doing it while they should be grinding at college to 'secure' their future. There is something scarier than walking a path of uncertainty; it is to see your kid do that. My family has watched it and backed me. If that is not support, what is?

To my friends at college—Rishi, Zain, Harsh, Arunaabh. Sitting in the library and writing this book, while everyone around spiked their grades and did crazy good things for their careers, would have been a lot scarier without you. Also, you guys are the people I have spent the most amazing time with. Thank you for being my gang and cheering me through and through.

To my friends back at home—Ginni, Medha, Ankit, Cyril, Sam, Aditya, Ankita, Samriddhi and Ayushi. The friendships that have stood the test of time. Thank you for sticking with me, and holding me through all these years.

To two of the most special teachers I have ever had—Mr. Alan Cowell and Mrs. Ipsita Sharan. Not only did you shape my craft, but also acknowledged the writer in me. You gave me the confidence to bring my art out in the world. Thank you.

To my first reader and the biggest cheerleader I have—Abhinav Raj. Thank you for reading all my first drafts, even if at times they looked like 20,000 words of trash. Thank you for giving me the most critical feedback always. You have seen and shaped my journey like no one else.

To my publishing team—thank you for bearing with my anxieties of publishing for the first time. And for turning my manuscript into such a beautiful book.

Lastly, if you have ever read something I have written and cheered for me, thank you.

ABOUT THE AUTHOR

Rahul Shandilya is a Mechanical Engineering undergraduate at BITS Pilani, Goa, who finds himself an artist at heart. He has been writing for more than nine years and has held several literary positions, like the chief editor of his school novel, IGNITE. *The Times of India* featured it as the first of its kind in the city. He has also won several poetry competitions across the country.

He finds stories a great way to express oneself while hiding behind characters, which explains his love for contemporary fiction. Rahul keeps experimenting with different poetry forms and writing styles. He likes to infuse new things into his native style to create something new.

When not writing, you can find him strumming his guitar or playing his keyboard. He sings okayish, loves deep, interesting conversations, and would die without coffee. *Nothing* is sometimes his favourite thing to do.

Connect with him:

Website: https://shandilyawrites.in/

Email: rahul@shandilyawrites.in